PLANETFALL

Sentinel of EARTH

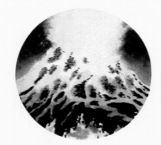

THE GREAT FEDERATION OF THE *INNER ACCORD* WAS FORMED, MANY CENTURIES AGO, BY A NUMBER OF PLANETS NEAR THE CENTRE OF THE GALAXY. THE WORLDS OF THE *ACCORD* NOW NUMBER EIGHTY-FOUR, AND ALL OF THEM CONTAIN ALIEN CIVILIZATIONS THAT ARE VERY ANCIENT, AND INCREDIBLY ADVANCED — BUT NOT JUST SCIENTIFICALLY.

THE BEINGS OF THOSE WORLDS LIVE ACCORDING TO DEEP-ROOTED BELIEFS IN PEACE, HARMONY, CO-OPERATION AND RESPECT FOR ALL FORMS OF LIFE. THERE IS NO CRIME ON THE WORLDS OF THE *INNER ACCORD*, NO MENTAL ILLNESS, NO UNREST OR DISRUPTION, NO ANTI-SOCIAL BEHAVIOUR OF ANY KIND.

ONE OF THE ORIGINAL MEMBERS OF THE *ACCORD* WAS THE PLANET *ABETHAZE*, *RASL CA'WRN'S* HOME WORLD. IT IS A BEAUTIFUL PLANET, BUT MUCH OF IT IS WILD AND DANGEROUS, WITH MANY AGGRESSIVE LIFE FORMS. YET THE CIVILIZED BEINGS OF *ABETHAZE* LIVE SERENELY ON THEIR WORLD WITHOUT EVER DEPARTING FROM ANY OF THE BELIEFS THAT GOVERN THE *INNER ACCORD*. (FOR A MORE DETAILED LOOK AT *ABETHAZE*, SEE PAGE *15*.).

BUT BEYOND THE WORLDS OF THE *ACCORD*, THERE ARE A GREAT MANY OTHER CIVILIZED PLANETS. MOST OF THEM ARE JUST AS ADVANCED IN THEIR SCIENCE — BUT NOT IN THEIR BELIEFS OR ATTITUDES. THOSE WORLDS PRODUCE A GOOD DEAL OF CRIME, VIOLENCE AND MISERY. THEY ALSO PRODUCE MANY INTERPLANETARY CRIMINALS, WHO ROAM THE *SPACEWAYS* LOOKING FOR LESS ADVANCED, DEFENCELESS WORLDS — LIKE *EARTH* — WHICH THEY CAN PREY UPON.

DATABRIEF 2 : THE SENTINEL'S PLEDGE.

FROM THE BEGINNING, THE ALIEN BEINGS OF THE *INNER ACCORD* WERE CONCERNED ABOUT THE LESS ADVANCED PLANETS OF THE GALAXY, WHICH WERE HELPLESS AGAINST INTERPLANETARY RAIDERS. BUT THE *ACCORD* COULD NOT CREATE ANY KIND OF MILITARY FORCE TO GUARD THOSE PLANETS, SINCE THAT WOULD BE AGAINST ALL THEIR BELIEFS. INSTEAD, THEY CREATED THE *SENTINELS*.

THE *SENTINELS* ARE VOLUNTEERS, FROM THE DIFFERENT WORLDS OF THE *ACCORD*. THERE ARE SELDOM VERY MANY OF THEM — USUALLY ONE OR TWO FOR EACH WORLD TO BE PROTECTED. YET IN MOST CASES THE *SENTINELS* PERFORM THEIR TASKS VERY SUCCESSFULLY. AND THEY DO SO MAINLY BY USING THEIR INTELLIGENCE AND QUICKNESS OF MIND, HELPED BY A FEW SPECIAL ABILITIES THAT SOME OF THEM HAVE, AND BY THE HIGH TECHNOLOGY OF THE *ACCORD*.

NOR DO ANY OF THOSE VOLUNTEERS EVER FORGET WHAT IS REQUIRED OF THEM, BY THE FORMAL *PLEDGE* THAT EACH OF THEM VOWS TO OBEY, WHEN HE BECOMES A *SENTINEL*.

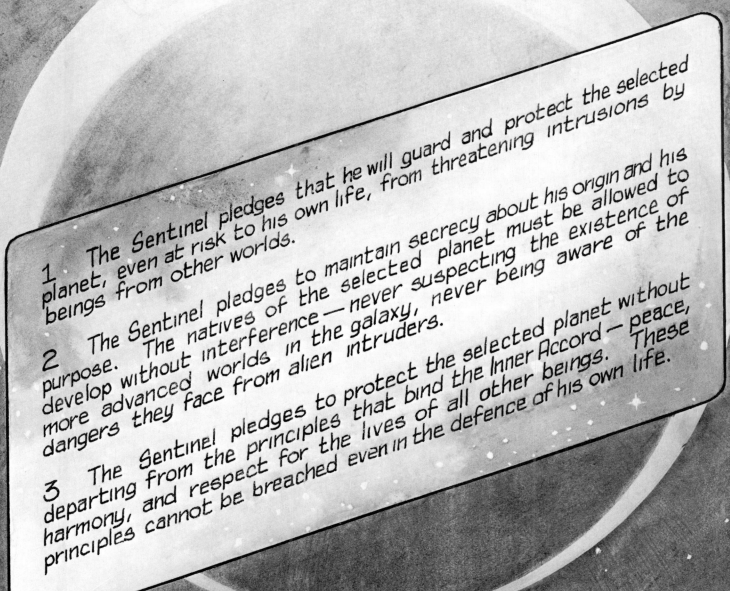

1 The Sentinel pledges that he will guard and protect the selected planet, even at risk to his own life, from threatening intrusions by beings from other worlds.

2 The Sentinel pledges to maintain secrecy about his origin and his purpose. The natives of the selected planet must be allowed to develop without interference — never suspecting the existence of more advanced worlds in the galaxy, never being aware of the dangers they face from alien intruders.

3 The Sentinel pledges to protect the selected planet without departing from the principles that bind the Inner Accord — peace, harmony, and respect for the lives of all other beings. These principles cannot be breached even in the defence of his own life.

1 Sentinel of EARTH — Rasl Ca'wrn

The flat metal disc beneath the feet of the dark-robed alien was less than a metre wide. But the alien balanced easily upon it, calm and untroubled, as it lifted him high into the soft, fragrant air.

Wisps of cloud drifted past him now and then as the disc wafted him upwards, and a gentle breeze ruffled the edges of his robe. He glanced around with interest and enjoyment, as his disc carried him past other floating discs—larger ones, hanging motionless in the air, like broad hovering platforms. On some of those platforms he saw other alien beings, in all the astonishing shapes that were produced by more than eighty planets.

Some sat in small groups, talking quietly. Others sat or stood alone, in private study or meditation. On one enormous disc, a group of aliens strolled through luxurious gardens, containing the splendid forms and colours of plants from a dozen worlds. On another platform, another alien group wandered among eerily beautiful works of art, also gathered from many worlds.

5

David Jackson.

All the hovering discs formed the Palace of Accord—a palace without walls or ceilings, without halls or chambers. A floating palace, high in a serene sky over a quiet turquoise sea. That sea existed on a silent planet—a world that offered a gentle climate but that had never produced life of any sort. It was the ideal site for the magnificent palace, where aliens from all the planets of the Inner Accord could meet, and mingle, and discuss events on their separate worlds.

The dark-robed being, on his small disc, had visited the Palace of Accord before—for the same purpose that had brought him there that day. Even so, he was affected just as deeply now as he had been the first time, by the beauty and tranquillity of the Palace. But as the disc rose still higher, he turned his gaze away from the wonders around him, looking up towards another floating platform, which was his goal.

On that platform, six more alien beings sat quietly on plain seats, placed in a semi-circle. The small disc carrying the dark-robed alien glided forward, then settled smoothly down on to the platform, so that the robed being stood in the centre of the semi-circle, facing the six.

One of the seated figures stirred slightly. 'Rasl Ca'wrn,' it said in a darkly husky voice. 'Welcome to the Gathering'.

The robed being, Rasl Ca'wrn, inclined his head politely, but said nothing. Silence gathered as he studied those in front of him, with friendly interest, and was studied by them in the same way.

Rasl Ca'wrn was tall, and thin to the point of boniness, though his four-fingered hands looked strong and capable. He was entirely hairless, and his skin was the colour of burnished gold. And his large, nearly black eyes, with their strange square pupils, held a look of quiet, calm intelligence and competence.

Of the six beings before him, three resembled Rasl in their shape and colouring, and wore similar dark robes. One of the other three was a narrow-bodied, large-headed being who seemed to be formed mostly of white metal. Another was rounded, covered in short fur, and faceless—its entire head sprouting delicate tendrils that waved ceaselessly. And the sixth, the one that had

spoken, was large and solid, with powerful tentacles reaching out from its gleaming-purple body.

After that brief pause, the tentacled one's husky voice spoke again.

'There has been a disturbance in the fabric of space,' it said. 'A small shifting of time lines and other forces. It has had no effect on the worlds of the Inner Accord, nor on any other planet in the galaxy, as far as we know.' The being leaned forward intently. 'But there has been an alteration of the Spaceways.'

'It has happened before,' the metal-bodied alien put in. 'The last time was several ages ago. It is merely an inconvenience.'

Rasl nodded, still remaining silent. The Spaceways, as he well knew, were special paths among the stars of the galaxy—the paths that were followed by spaceships moving unimaginably faster than the speed of light.

When the ships reached that speed, a complex energy field caused them to disappear from the 'real' space of the galaxy, and to enter a 'non-space'. Then they could flit, in just a few days, across distances that a beam of light could not cover in millions of years.

But in that 'non-space', the ships had to follow the paths that were precisely mapped—or they might never return into 'real' space. They had to follow the Spaceways.

'Two of the major Spaceways,' the tentacled speaker continued, 'now reach out towards the fringe of the galaxy. In that region, ships must travel briefly through *normal* space—to cross from one of the Spaceways to the other. As they do so, they will pass very near to a system of ten planets around a small yellow star.'

Still Rasl waited, knowing what was coming.

'One of those planets bears intelligent life,' the speaker said. 'It is not very advanced—it has only crude and limited space flight, and no notion of how populated the galaxy is. So that planet is dangerously exposed, to the more . . . unpleasant travellers of the Spaceways.'

For the first time, Rasl Ca'wrn spoke, in a voice that was as calm as his expression. 'It needs a Sentinel.'

The purplish being lifted a tentacle in agreement. 'Because of your successes elsewhere, Rasl, you have been selected as Sentinel for this planet. If you accept.'

'Of course,' Rasl said at once.

The alien who was partly made of metal produced a creaking noise that might have been laughter. 'It always amuses me,' it told Rasl, 'that so many of you citizens of the planet Abethaze volunteer to be Sentinels. As if you did not have hardship enough, surviving by peaceful means on your own harsh world.'

One of the other golden-skinned beings, among the group of six, smiled and nodded his smooth head. 'Perhaps it is because we are taught by our world what is the truth of the matter,' he said. 'That it takes a peace-lover—to keep the peace.'

Rasl Ca'wrn smiled as a ripple of strange sounds, also laughter, passed through the group.

'Now,' the tentacled being went on, 'you will need only small alterations to resemble a native of this planet. As usual, you will be given full knowledge of the place, including its main languages, at hypno-speed. You will have a fully equipped spaceship, and any other materials you may need.' The tentacles

waved briefly. 'And we have selected a companion for you, if you approve. I believe you know him—Mizzo, of the planet Crek-laty.'

Rasl's grin was wide and merry. 'I know Mizzo. I approve, with pleasure.'

'Excellent,' the other said. 'Then you may begin your preparations at once. But first, of course, there is the necessary formality of the Pledge.'

'Of course,' Rasl said again, with not a hint of impatience.

'Very well,' the other said. 'Rasl Ca'wrn, we of the Gathering of Elder Sentinels ask you to call to your mind the Sentinel's Pledge—and to undertake once again to keep to the ways of the Inner Accord, in all your actions on the planet that you will serve.'

'Hardly necessary, for someone from Abethaze,' muttered the metallic alien, with a slight creak.

'I so pledge,' Rasl replied firmly.

The tentacled alien sat back with an air of satisfaction. 'Excellent. The good wishes of this Gathering go with you, in your new task.'

'Thank you,' Rasl said, inclining his head in another slight bow.

At an unseen signal, the invisible energies within the small disc, under his feet, came to life. Gently, smoothly, the disc began to raise him from the surface of the platform.

But then he halted it, as the metallic being creaked once more with laughter.

'You have not asked the planet's name, Rasl,' the alien said. 'It is amusing in its lack of originality. Like all natives of backward planets, the creatures believe themselves to be special and unique in the universe. They have called their world . . . Earth.'

Rasl smiled slightly. 'It is a good enough name. No doubt it is a good enough world.'

Then the disc resumed its rise, curving silently away and down from the platform holding the seated group.

At almost exactly the same moment, halfway across the galaxy, a dark and weirdly shaped spacecraft was moving silently through the interstellar emptiness. It held only one occupant, a creature that seemed to be merely a shapeless mass—its short, powerful arms and legs almost hidden within a tangled covering of long black hair. The face, too, was almost hidden—except for a glint of pointed teeth, and the narrow slits of two yellow eyes.

The eyes widened slightly, seeming to glow with an eerie light of their own, as the creature leaned forward to look again at the screen of the ship's navigation computer. For some hours, the creature had been studying the strange shapes flashing on to the screen. Now, at last, it seemed satisfied. It snarled softly through its sharp teeth, and the shaggy mass of hair quivered, as if in anticipation.

'A shift in the Spaceways,' it said to itself, in a low voice that was like a growl. 'New paths to follow. New worlds for Ekridolak to plunder.'

It snarled again, and stretched out a hairy arm. Muscular fingers, tipped with curving claws, flickered over the controls, to send the weird ship flashing away, along a different route among the stars.

CAN ONE STRANGE BEING — OR EVEN TWO — PROTECT THE ENTIRE PLANET EARTH FROM DEADLY ALIEN INTRUDERS? THE STORY OF THE SENTINEL CONTINUES ON PAGE 16.

Can *you* suRvive on an aLiéN PlaneT?

eeee . . . . **eeee** . . . . **eeee** . . . . You are awoken abruptly by the sound of the great spaceliner's emergency siren, you roll out of your bunk and into the service corridor . . . . **eeee** . . . . **eeee** . . . . emergency lighting only, must be a massive power drain, has to be main drive failure, nothing else could suck in power like that . . . . **eeee** . . . . **eeee** . . . . more awake now, you see the soft red warning flashing on the bulkhead . . . . **'Life Support Decay' 'Life Support Decay'** . . . , the sickening realization hits you, the massive spaceship has been holed . . . . **eeee** . . . . **eeee** . . . . **eeeeeeeeeeeeeeeeeeeeeeeeeeeeeeeeeeeeeeeeeeeeeeeeee** the tone denotes decay of main system integrity . . . , life support will fail in one hundred and eighty seconds . . . you have three minutes to reach an EGG, one of the ship's life capsules, or you're dead . . . . **eeeeeeeeeeeeeeeeeeeeeeeeee** . . . two capsules in your section, one forward, one aft . . . no chance forward . . . you turn back, groping, half-running, half-stumbling . . . you will have thirty seconds when the siren stops, you can almost feel the precious air leaking out of the ship . . . **eeeeeeeeeeeeeeeeeeeeeeeeeeeee**———————————

Turn over to see if you escaped from the doomed spaceliner ...

Can *you* SURVive on än aLieN PlaneT?

You awaken in an unfamiliar cocoon-like atmosphere, a green winking light in front of you. No, not a light – a vizi-screen. It is warm and your body is supported by a contoured couch. You made it. You are in the EGG and the EGG has already landed. Standard procedure of course; the EGG will have put you to sleep on ejection from the stricken ship and woken you only after a safe landing, and only if there is a chance of imminent rescue or . . . you look up suddenly at the vizi-screen to find your worst fears confirmed . . . or if the escape capsule has landed on **unstable terrain** . . . the briefing by the EGG's computer is chillingly stark . . . **METEORITE DISABLED AND PUNCTURED SHIP** . . . the EGG's brain would have been updated by the main ship's computer right up to the last seconds . . . **only available landing site planet ABETHAZE** . . . **life capsule has landed in southern hemisphere** . . . **planet ABETHAZE oxygen/nitrogen breathable atmosphere** . . . **landing surface swamp** . . . **life capsule sinking** . . . **you have twenty minutes to abandon capsule** . . . **local data follows** . . . **equipment inventory on capsule follows** . . . You stare at the screen in horror. Not only will you have to abandon the EGG within ten minutes because it has landed in a bog, but you have been stranded on the most notorious planet in the known galaxy – notorious for the sheer ferocity of its native lifeforms . . .

Can You Survive On This Deadly Alien Planet?

1 You have TEN MINUTES before your Escape Capsule (Egg) sinks beneath the alien swamp. **DON'T WASTE TIME!**

2 Call up the *Alien Lifeform Data* on the Egg's computer, see page 96. You can look at the screen for FIVE MINUTES ONLY. Knowledge of the local lifeforms could save your life. **DO THIS NOW!**

3 Choose four pieces of equipment from the *Escape Capsule Survival Kit* (The Eggbox). See page 14. Mark your choices on your Survival Chart. **SEVEN MINUTES AND COUNTING.**

4 You have 50 *Survival Points* to start with as shown on your *Survival Chart*. During your attempt to survive on Abethaze you may lose survival points. If your survival points should ever fall to 'O' or below then you have failed to survive this time and must start again. You will be told how many survival points to lose as you go along. **SIX MINUTES AND COUNTING.**

5 Now turn to page 25 to see the deadly Alien Swamp that awaits you outside the capsule. The *Alien Swamp* has a number of Action Boxes. You must choose in each case what to do next. Using your knowledge of the local lifeforms and watching the scene before you, you must decide which action to take. Remember you don't have much time to think on Abethaze. **FIVE MINUTES AND COUNTING.**

6 Make your choice of action on the Survival Chart (Example: in Action Box 1 you must decide to 'Run' or 'Stand still'. If you decide to 'Run' then mark 'B' in the answer box. Complete ALL the Action Boxes for the Alien scene. **FOUR MINUTES AND COUNTING.**

7 Now turn to the page following the Alien scene you are looking at to discover how well you survived its perils. (Examples: if you decided to 'Run' in Action Box 1 then you must look at Result Box 1 B to see what happened to you.) If you are told to lose survival points then cross off survival points on your Survival Chart accordingly. **THREE MINUTES AND COUNTING.**

8 Provided you are still alive (have more than 'O' survival points) now continue on to see how well you survive the sinister *Alien Glade*. Turn to page 48. You must start the *Alien Glade* with the same amount of survival points as you finished the *Alien Swamp*. **TWO MINUTES AND COUNTING.**

9 Follow steps 6–10 for the *Alien Glade* and then the spectacular *Alien Night*. Turn to page 80. **SIXTY SECONDS AND COUNTING.**

10 If you have survived the deadly *Alien Swamp*, *Alien Glade* and *Alien Night* turn to page 92 to see if you will be rescued. **ABANDON THE EGG.**

SURVIVAL CHART

SPACE ACADEMY SURVIVAL RATING

Cross off survival points as you lose them from the top down and then **IF YOU SURVIVE** read off your rating.

50	NATIVE ABETHAZIAN
45	HIGHEST RECORDED HUMAN
40	ACADEMY ROLL OF HONOUR
35	GRANDMASTER SURVIVOR
30	MASTER SURVIVOR
25	CADET SURVIVOR
20	SURVIVAL RETRAINING ESSENTIAL
15	THREE MONTHS REST AND RECUPERATION
10	BARELY ALIVE
5	GIBBERING WRECK (Hospitalized for life)
0	DID NOT SURVIVE

You may choose **four** pieces of equipment to take with you from the Escape Capsule Survival Kit—this is the standard equipment carried by all Space Navy E99 capsules. Choose your equipment with care. The wrong equipment will be useless dead weight to carry around with you. The correct equipment could save your life! Remember you can only choose *four* pieces of equipment—you are not able to carry more than this. Give some thought also to how you will get off this terrible planet if you do manage to survive. How will you get help? When you have finished reading this you have only *FIVE MINUTES* to choose the equipment. Mark what you choose on a piece of paper.
YOU NOW HAVE EIGHT MINUTES LEFT BEFORE THE CAPSULE GOES UNDER. RETURN IMMEDIATELY TO STEP 3 OF THE EMERGENCY DRILL.

1 SUBSPACE DISTRESS BEACON

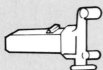

Once activated, this beacon sends out a signal to any spacecraft within a range of ten light years.

2 PORTABLE LASER   NO UNAUTHORIZED USE.

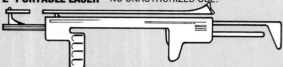

For use on planets with a hostility grading of 1000+ only. Effective beam range of 500 marks.

3 STANDARD ISSUE SPACE KNIFE

Pavan molecular blade.

4 EXTRA VEHICULAR ACTIVITY BOOTS

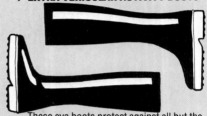

These eva boots protect against all but the sharpest projectiles.

5 RESPIRATOR

Protects wearer against breathing poison gas. Oxygen for 3 hours continuous use.

6 RESCUE FLARE

Suitable for use in atmosphere or in space. Visible from 1000 units. Flare lasts one hour.

7 TRADING KIT

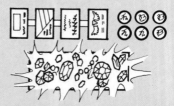

Contains precious metals, gemstones and other minerals considered valuable in over fifty star systems for use in trade, barter or payment with intelligent life-forms.

8 SPACESUIT

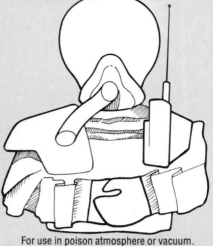

For use in poison atmosphere or vacuum. Offers complete protection but can be punctured by sharp projectile. Oxygen and nutrition for 12 hours continuous use.

9 IMAGE INTENSIFIERS

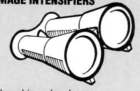

These binocular glasses enable the user to see at night.

10 PHOTON TORCH

Wide beam hand torch for use at night.

11 MEDIKIT

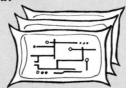

Dispensable computerized medical repair kit. Apply directly to injury. The kit will automatically diagnose and treat any damage to your body. Ineffective against major injury. Each medikit contains three pads. Each pad can only be used once.

12 RADIATION GLASSES

For use where visible radiation may damage eyesight.

13 HI-NUTRI-PAC

Each pack contains ten daily survival rations for one person.

14 PORKY-PORTABLE RECREATION COMPANION

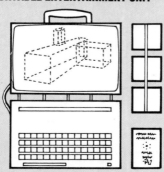

Fully personalized survival companion for survivor stranded over long period including sense of humour (new jokes guaranteed) and psychological morale booster.

15 PORTABLE ENTERTAINMENT UNIT

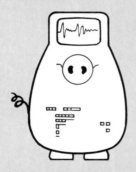

Full holographic/Audio visual entertainment unit. Complete library of holos and di-book for long term survival entertainment.

The inhabitants were, in their primitive origins, gatherers but never hunters, since they were (and are) vegetarian and non-aggressive. Those forebears had a mystic/religious reverence for life and for nature, like the affinity with the land shown by some American Indians. Today, the highly civilized Abethazians retain that reverence, and have developed it into a philosophy that was of major importance to forming the Inner Accord.

The planet has several large land masses and a great deal of ocean. The Abethazians keep their population at a level that can easily be supported by one land mass, which has a temperate climate and a variety of fertile landscapes. They have reached a high level of science and technology, which they use to enhance their peaceful, 'natural' life style. They build no cities, but live in roomy settlements that blend with the semi-wild terrain. They use their world's natural resources, but do not exploit or exhaust them, and take great pains to leave the landscape undisturbed. Even their sole spaceport is on a rocky plateau among bleak mountains almost devoid of life forms.

The exploiting, expanding urges of humanity (born of greed and aggression) have never existed on Abethaze. So the other land masses are still almost entirely wild and 'natural', with only a few scattered outposts of Abethazians on them (for scientific study and careful resource-gathering). All the land masses support a startling number of dangerous life forms, including the one where most of the population lives – but the people use a gentle form of force field as protection, which halts or diverts an attacking beast without harming it. If an Abethazian is killed by some vicious life form, it is seen as a tragic accident, like a death from some lethal virus. The Abethazians seek where they can to 'immunize' themselves, against both their viruses and their monsters. The human way of razing and 'settling' the wilderness, and hunting and slaughtering wild life, would be to them entirely horrible

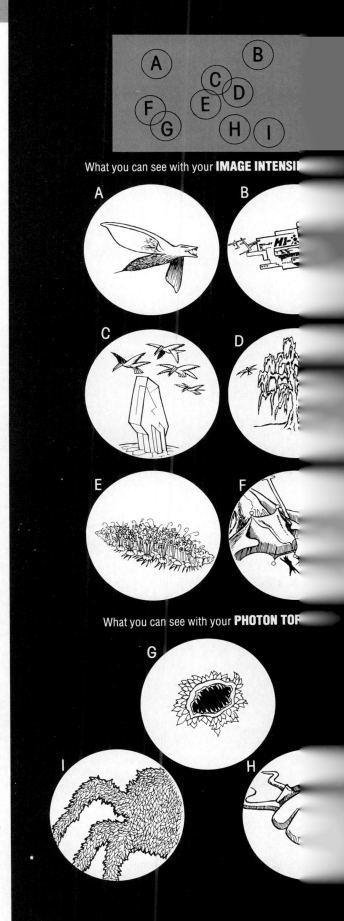

What you can see with your **IMAGE INTENSI**

What you can see with your **PHOTON TOR**

2 The Listeners

Russell Carron stepped out of his car, and glanced up and down the street. It was a small, ordinary street in a small, ordinary town—a street of well-kept houses and tidy gardens, of thick hedges and firmly closed net curtains. On one side stood a terrace of narrow, two-storey houses, and Russell had parked in front of the house on the end, which had recently become his home. Across the street were a number of larger houses, semi-detached, with well-tended lawns and gardens. And at that time, in the middle of that Sunday morning, not a single person was visible on either side of the quiet street.

It was an ideal place for Russell to live, and had been chosen for that reason. His neighbours had shown only a little curiosity about him at first, during sociable but very brief chats on the street or in the local shops. They had soon found him to be a friendly but quiet young man, even rather dull, who kept himself to himself. And his neighbours were happy to let him do so, and now seldom paid much attention to him—which was just how he wanted it.

But at that moment two of his younger neighbours were paying a great deal of attention to him, though he did not know it. Russell had not seen the two children, crouching within only a few metres of his car. Playing some imaginative game, they had crept into the small square of Russell's front garden, before his car had arrived. Now they were squeezed tightly against the dense hedge, hoping to avoid the embarrassment of being caught there.

Russell turned back towards his car, stooping to reach inside. He looked as ordinary as everything else on that street, with a pleasant but unremarkable face, short brown hair and calm brown eyes. The only unusual thing about him was that he was quite tall, and very thin—yet he moved easily, without awkwardness, and there was a look of wiry strength in his lean body and his long-fingered hands. And those hands were lifting, from the car, an extremely ordinary cardboard box, of the sort that groceries are carried in.

But then, surprisingly, he spoke to the box. 'Enjoy your outing?' he said.

Even more surprisingly, the box seemed to reply. 'Outing?' it said, in a light voice that held an edge of sharpness. 'Inside a box, and then inside that primitive machine? You make me a prisoner.'

Russell grinned as he carried the box towards his front door. 'Not half an hour ago you were chasing a butterfly through the woods, like a yearling.'

The voice from the box chuckled. 'A pretty thing it was. When can we go again?'

'In a day or two,' Russell said. He unlocked his front door and stepped inside, clicking the door shut behind him.

The two children by the hedge, whom he had walked past without seeing, stared at each other with astonishment. Silently, without a word, they began to creep forward towards the front window of the house, partly masked by a lilac bush just beginning to bloom.

Inside the house, in the main downstairs room, Russell placed the box on the solid wooden table that stood in the centre. And from the box an amazing creature emerged. At first glance it seemed to be a large lizard, more than a metre long from nose to tail. But no lizard like it had ever lived on Earth.

Its hide was not scaly, but covered with very short fur, smooth and soft, its colour mingling pleasant tones of brown and green. The head seemed slightly too large for the body, and there was a clear light of intelligence in its bright violet eyes.

The creature sat up, braced on its sturdy tail. With its forefeet, which had opposing thumbs like human hands, it scratched luxuriously at its slightly rounded belly.

'It is stuffy in here,' it announced in its light, edged voice, 'and I am hungry.'

'Mizzo,' Russell said with a mock-sigh, 'you're always hungry.'

As he spoke, he moved to the window, since the room was indeed stuffy in the warmth of a June morning. As he raised the window a few centimetres, he did not see the two children ducking down among the lilac leaves. Nor did he notice that he had left the curtains ruffled and slightly parted.

'Is there chocolate?' asked the creature whose name was Mizzo. 'Or the crispy things?'

'They're called crisps, as you know very well,' Russell said, 'and you ate the last of them yesterday. You also know that too much chocolate puts you to sleep for hours.'

'Why not sleep?' Mizzo grumbled.

'There is little else to do. And tonight no doubt it will be staring at the picture machine, as always.'

'The television is a good way to add to our knowledge,' Russell told him.

Mizzo snorted. 'Knowledge! What I see on it I do not understand, much of the time. And I believe that the people here also cannot understand. They watch and watch, night upon night, hoping that understanding will sometime come.' He yawned, slim forked tongue flickering. 'It is a planet of dimwits, my friend, as boring as . . .'

His voice broke off. A faint sound had come from the direction of the window, and Russell had stiffened with alarm. Soundlessly he mouthed the words 'keep talking' at Mizzo, then turned and ambled idly towards the side of the room.

Mizzo blinked his violet eyes, understanding. 'What is worst,' he went on in the same grumbling tone, 'is that we see pictures of places that might be interesting, but we cannot go to see them. Here you keep me, within these brick walls, or else you put me in a box and call it an 'outing'. I tell you, I am in prison . . .'

Again his voice tailed off. Out of sight of the window, Russell had moved swiftly to the front door, opening it silently. He made no sound as he stepped outside, on to the small patch of grass, facing the lilac bush at his front window.

'Hello,' he said quietly.

The two children started and whirled, from where they had been peering tensely through the partly open window. Their faces went ashy white, and they pressed themselves back against the house, trembling as if they were about to leap into headlong flight.

But they could not flee. The thick hedge extended along the side of the house as well as the front, and their only path of escape was blocked by the tall shape of the man looming in front of them.

'Don't be frightened,' Russell said. 'I won't hurt you.'

'You leave us alone,' quavered one of the children—a girl, about ten years old, in jeans and sweatshirt, with a mop of black curls. 'Or I'll tell my dad.'

'Her dad's a police inspector,' the other child said, also in a shaky voice. He was a red-haired, sturdy boy—about the same size and age, and dressed much the same, as his companion.

Russell sighed. Worse and worse, he thought to himself. 'Don't be afraid,' he repeated. 'I'll stay just where I am. I only want to know why you were at my window.'

The two children stared at him, seeming to take a little courage from his quiet voice, and from the fact that he seemed calm, relaxed, unthreatening.

'You're an *alien*!' the girl suddenly burst out. 'From another *planet*!'

'And so's that talking lizard in there!' the boy added.

Though Russell's face did not change, his heart sank. The children had seen and heard everything. He had allowed the quiet dullness of his life, since coming to that house, to lull him into a moment's carelessness. And now the Pledge had been broken, and everything was at risk.

He forced himself to smile. 'Surely you don't believe in things like aliens?' he said.

Growing braver by the moment, the children looked insulted, as children do when they are treated like infants. 'Sure we do,' the girl said. 'We read space stories all the time.'

'And my dad's a teacher,' the boy said, 'and he says there're prob'ly *lots* of aliens out in space . . .' He paused, as a fearful new thought struck him. 'Are there more of you, round here?'

'Are you invading Earth?' the girl asked. Both their voices had grown shaky again.

'*No*,' Russell said firmly, at once. Then he too paused, studying the children thoughtfully. It was clear that he could not bluff them—they had seen and heard too much. But there might be a way to salvage something, to restore some of the secrecy demanded in the Pledge.

'Listen,' he went on at last. 'No matter what you heard through the window, right now I'm just what you see—an ordinary man. And I'm not going to harm you, or anyone. Believe me, it's impossible for me to harm any living thing, intentionally.'

The children merely stared at him, tense and wary.

Russell sighed again. 'The fact is that *you* could do a lot of harm to *me*—and, in a way, to the Earth. I'd like to tell you about it, make you see that I'm not dangerous. But we can't stand here like this. I don't suppose you'd come into the house?'

The children looked even more wary, and quickly shook their heads.

'I thought not.' Russell hesitated for a moment. 'Here's what I'll do. *I'll* go into the house. I'll get some water and a cloth, and come out and wash my car. While I'm gone, if you want, you can run away. But if you're willing to let me explain things to you, you can stay around—at a safe distance—and hear what I have to say.'

Without a pause, he turned and strode into the house.

Mizzo's bright eyes swung towards him. 'Is this a sensible action?' the little alien asked. 'Should I not have come and frightened them into keeping silence. . .?'

'It wouldn't work,' Russell said briefly. 'Better to befriend them, if we can.'

But what if I can't? he asked himself, as he went to the kitchen. Of course, if they run off, going home full of tales of aliens and talking lizards, the adults would probably not believe them. But what if that police-inspector father should decide just to keep an eye on the newcomer to the street? What if others heard the tales, and grew curious?

It was the last thing he wanted—humans growing curious about him, watching him, investigating him. There would be much more risk, then, that one day someone else might see something strange, mysterious . . . *alien*.

No, he thought miserably. If they run away, I will have to leave Earth. Another will have to be prepared, to come in my place. And before he can get here, the Earth will be left unguarded . . .

He emerged from the kitchen with a bucket of water and a cloth, and left the house. And the tension went out of him in a huge sigh of relief.

The children were still there. They were standing on the pavement, near his car, poised and nervous as if they might flee at any moment like frightened deer. But they were there.

Russell smiled at them, and walked to his car, careful not to go too near to the anxious pair. Then, like any ordinary suburbanite on a Sunday, he began to wash the car. And as he did so, he talked, so that only the children could hear.

He made their eyes widen with a brief account of the civilized worlds of the Inner Accord, and the less civilized planets beyond it. He astonished them with the story of how Rasl Ca'wrn became Russell Carron. He told them of the shift in the Spaceways, which exposed Earth to space-travelling evil-doers. And he told them finally of the Sentinels, and their task on the worlds that they guarded.

As he spoke, the children began to edge closer, listening intently. The wariness began to leave their eyes, and their faces became alive with excitement and wonder. It seemed that they were believing him—that they felt they could trust him. And that had much to do with the quiet steadiness of his voice, the calm friendliness of his eyes.

'So you see,' he said at last, 'a great deal depends on my secret staying a secret. Otherwise I'd have to leave Earth. And before another Sentinel gets here—to some other town—your world could be in danger.'

The children looked at him, as if thinking hard, then looked at each other. Finally the dark-haired girl took a step towards Russell, holding out her hand, with a small smile.

'You left the rear window streaky—Mr Carron,' she said.

Russell blinked, puzzled, and handed her the wet cloth. 'Call me Russell,' he said. 'Or Russ.'

'I'm Lindy Brown,' the girl said, turning away to polish the rear window. 'And he's Jeff Asher.'

'We live over there,' Jeff said, pointing across the street to two houses, three doors apart.

'Does this mean you believe me?' Russell asked quietly.

Again the children looked at each other, and then they nodded. 'It's kind of hard to take in, all at once,' Lindy said. 'But we believe you. And we won't tell a single other person. We promise.'

'We could *help* you!' Jeff said eagerly.

'Perhaps,' Russell said, smiling. 'But some of the aliens who might come here can be very dangerous. And they might land anywhere on Earth.'

'How can you know when they land?' Jeff asked.

'I have a ship orbiting Earth,' Russell explained. 'There's a force screen around it, so it's invisible to any kind of detector. But it can spot any alien ship approaching Earth. And it lets me know if one lands—through this.' He held out his left hand, with a heavy, ornate ring on the middle finger. 'I call it my AID—Alien Intruder Detector.'

The children stared at the ring with interest. Then Lindy looked up, her brow furrowed. 'But how can you guard Earth if you don't believe in shooting the evil aliens, or anything?'

'It depends,' Russell said vaguely. 'There can be many ways.'

Jeff's brow also creased. 'Isn't there some kind of Galactic Patrol, or something, like in the books?'

Russell shook his head. 'Most of the worlds beyond the Inner Accord have their own peace-keeping forces, but only on each planet. Those other worlds fear that if they set up an *interplanetary* force, some evil characters might take it over, and use it to build an empire.' He smiled ruefully. 'And on the worlds of the Inner Accord, every citizen is a peace-keeper. Setting up any kind of police or military *force* is against our

nature. All we could do was create my small group—those beings, not very many of us, who are willing to serve as Sentinels.'

Lindy pursed her lips disapprovingly. 'It seems . . . silly, somehow, to expect you to guard the whole Earth, all by yourself.'

'But I'm not by myself,' Russell said with a smile. 'Why don't you come in and meet Mizzo? I think we could all do with a cool drink after so much talking.'

So the children followed him, excitedly, into the house—fully trusting him now, he knew with relief. But inside, the children paused, staring at the lizard-shape of Mizzo with some nervousness. And Mizzo gazed at them just as fixedly—before turning to Russell with a flicker of his narrow tongue.

'They speak as they feel,' Mizzo said.

'Mizzo is from the planet Crek-laty,' Russell told the children. 'He has a special ability to sense whether most other beings are telling the truth. He knows that we can trust you to keep our secret.'

The children nodded solemnly. 'We promised,' Jeff said.

'Also you might mention,' Mizzo put in, 'the resemblance I have to the dragons of this world's stories.' Startlingly, he huffed a short, sharp breath—which came out in a small burst of bright orange fire.

The children were enchanted. And within moments they were all sitting together, relaxed and happy, while Lindy and Jeff plied Mizzo with eager questions, and sipped at fizzy drinks provided by Russell. Mizzo was enjoying the attention, and also the drink, which he liked as much as chocolate and crisps.

'Excellent things to eat, on this world,' he announced cheerfully, and they all laughed and relaxed even more.

Until Russell started very slightly, and a strange blankness came over his face. He got up, muttered something about getting more drinks, and left the room. The children, chattering merrily, barely noticed. But Mizzo's violet eyes watched him intently, all the way out the door.

Russell did not go to the kitchen for more drinks. His expression had changed because of a feeling in his left hand. A firm squeezing pressure, as if the ring he wore—his AID—had suddenly become smaller. And he knew very well what that signal meant.

He hurried upstairs to his room, drew the curtains, made an adjustment to the ring, then held up his hand as if pointing the ring at the blank wall. A beam of light sprang from the ring, and—as a film projector throws images on a screen—a stream of figures appeared on the wall. With them were lines of writing in the language of Russell's home planet, Abethaze.

Russell studied the images for several long moments. He seemed to stiffen as he did so, and his expression grew even more bleakly empty. Then the images vanished, and he turned—moving slowly, as if very weary—and went back downstairs.

'Lindy, Jeff,' he said, as he re-entered the main room. 'I'm sorry, but we'll have to continue this another time. There's . . . I have some things I must do.'

Mizzo was still watching Russell steadily, and the children turned to him as well, surprised. They saw the change in his stance and his expression—and alarm sprang into their eyes as they guessed.

'There's some danger, isn't there?' Lindy asked quickly. 'One of those aliens that you're here to stop . . . ?'

Mizzo chuckled. 'They perceive clearly, these young ones.'

Russell was nodding. 'A great deal of danger. So I have to ask you both . . . to stay away for a while. Don't come anywhere near me, or this house, for some time.'

The words made Mizzo blink very rapidly, several times. But the children frowned. 'Why not?' Jeff asked.

'Because the danger is *here*,' Russell said heavily. 'The alien intruder is somewhere very near. Somewhere in this town.'

BEFORE YOU INVESTIGATE WHETHER ANY OF THE PEOPLE ON YOUR *STREET ARE ALIENS* —FRIENDLY OR OTHERWISE— CONTINUE THE STORY OF THE SENTINEL ON PAGE 44.

Can *you* SURVIVE on an aLIEN PlaneT?

1 YOU STEP OUT OF YOUR CAPSULE. IMMEDIATELY ONE OF THE FIERCE FLYING CREATURES SWOOPS DOWN AT YOU . . .

WILL YOU STAND STILL? (A)
WILL YOU RUN? (B)

2 WILL YOU WADE THROUGH THE LIQUID?

WILL YOU WALK ON THE MUDFLATS? (B)

3 SUDDENLY THE TUSK-BEASTS CHARGE AT YOU. HOW WILL YOU DEAL WITH THEM?

FIRE YOUR **LASER** (IF YOU HAVE ONE). (A)
STAND YOUR GROUND. (B)
FIRE A **RESCUE FLARE** (IF YOU HAVE ONE). (C)

24

The SWAMP..............

4

YOU WILL PASS CLOSE TO THESE BEAUTIFUL FERN-LIKE PLANTS THAT GROW ON THE MUDFLATS.

WILL YOU WALK VERY CAREFULLY PAST THEM? (A)
WILL YOU RUN PAST QUICKLY? (B)
WILL YOU WAIT UNTIL THE TUSK-BEAST HAS GONE PAST? (C)

Answer Box

Mark your choice of action here

△ 1	○ 2	▢ 3	⬡ 4

1A

1B

YOU KNOW THAT THE EARWING USES ITS EARS TO HUNT. IT SWOOPS PAST YOU TO CAPTURE A CREATURE LESS INTELLIGENT THAN YOURSELF.

THE EARWING CREATURE USES ITS EARS TO HUNT AND HEARING YOU RUNNING SWERVES FROM ITS ORIGINAL PREY TO ATTACK YOU! YOU JUST MANAGE TO FIGHT IT OFF WITH YOUR HANDS AND REGAIN THE SINKING CAPSULE. YOU LEAVE AGAIN IMMEDIATELY. *LOSE 5 SURVIVAL POINTS.*

2A

2B

THE TREES HAVE ROOTS THAT SPEAR UNDERWATER CREATURES FOR SUSTENANCE. ONE ROOT PIERCES YOUR LEG. THE INJURY, THOUGH NOT FATAL, IS VERY PAINFUL AND WILL HAMPER YOUR PROGRESS. USE A **MEDIKIT** OR *LOSE 7 SURVIVAL POINTS.*

THE MUDFLATS ARE SAFE ENOUGH TO WALK ON BUT THE CLOUDS OF GAS ARE POISONOUS. IF YOU DID NOT BRING THE **RESPIRATOR** OR THE **SPACESUIT** THEN THE GAS MAKES YOU DIZZY. *LOSE 4 SURVIVAL POINTS.*

3A

YOU FIRE YOUR LASER AND HIT THE HERD LEADER. THE TELEPATHIC BOND LINKING THE HERD IS BROKEN. FOR A MOMENT THE HERD WILL BE QUITE MAD. YOU ARE TRAMPLED UNDER FOOT. *LOSE 25 SURVIVAL POINTS.*

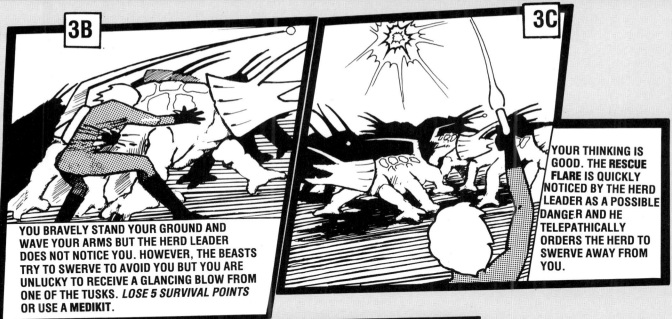

3B

YOU BRAVELY STAND YOUR GROUND AND WAVE YOUR ARMS BUT THE HERD LEADER DOES NOT NOTICE YOU. HOWEVER, THE BEASTS TRY TO SWERVE TO AVOID YOU BUT YOU ARE UNLUCKY TO RECEIVE A GLANCING BLOW FROM ONE OF THE TUSKS. *LOSE 5 SURVIVAL POINTS OR USE A MEDIKIT.*

3C

YOUR THINKING IS GOOD. THE **RESCUE FLARE** IS QUICKLY NOTICED BY THE HERD LEADER AS A POSSIBLE DANGER AND HE TELEPATHICALLY ORDERS THE HERD TO SWERVE AWAY FROM YOU.

4A TOO SLOW! THE DEADLY FERN-LIKE PLANT FIRES ITS SPORES AT YOU. THERE ARE TOO MANY FOR YOU TO SURVIVE. YOUR STAY ON ABETHAZE ENDS HERE.

4C

YOU WAIT AND ARE REWARDED AS A TUSK-BEAST LUMBERS PAST THE CLUMP OF FERNS. THE PLANT FIRES A SHOWER OF DARTS AT THE BEAST. MOST BOUNCE OFF ITS TOUGH SKIN. YOU WALK QUICKLY AND SAFELY PAST THE PLANT BEFORE IT HAS A CHANCE TO RELOAD.

4B

YOU'RE QUICK BUT NOT QUITE QUICK ENOUGH. A FEW OF THE DEADLY SPORES EMBED THEMSELVES IN YOUR ARM. IF YOU HAVE A **MEDIKIT** YOU CAN DESTROY THEM WITH NO ILL EFFECTS. OTHERWISE YOU WILL HAVE TO PULL THEM OUT. *LOSE 8 SURVIVAL POINTS.*

» PLaiN MAGIc «

by Tamora Pierce

For once I didn't have to steal the chance to talk to the peddler-woman who had set up shop in our village square. My parents *ordered* me to find out more about her. My mother hesitated, at first—she said a woman peddling alone was probably not respectable. In the end my father silenced her, saying, 'We must find out all we can. With a dragon about, any stranger is suspicious.'

That didn't make any sense to me, but I kept my mouth shut. Usually my father beat me for talking to strangers about the places they had been. I was the headman's daughter. I had to save all my attention for my village, not the world outside.

Hah!

When I got to the square, she had already put her goods out on a great tray that swung down from the side of her cart. She wasn't much to look at—brown and dry and thin, a little over thirty, maybe—but she made up for her plainness with the things she had to sell: bolts of cloth in a thousand colours, the finest lace I'd ever seen, dolls of any imaginable type, knotted bags in all sizes, braided rugs.

I told her my name—Tonya—and she gave hers, Lindri. It was easy enough to get her talking. I asked questions about what she had to sell, and she answered me. She even showed me the compact loom that fitted inside her cart and could be taken out and made larger. She brought out bags and baskets of threads and trims for me to look at, and allowed me to turn her spinning wheel a couple of times.

She was always busy with some bit of work, even while she talked to me. She started with a piece of lace, her needles darting through the strands of thread as if they lived on their own. I had never been very interested in needlework, but the way she did it made it seem interesting—fascinating, even. I was staring at the lace growing rapidly in her hands until she laughed and patted my cheek smartly, shaking me from a daze.

'Don't watch so long,' she said, grinning. 'They say there's a plain kind of magic in needlework—do you want to end up a slave to it forever, like me?'

'Are you?' I wanted to know. To me the idea that there could be magic in bits of string and rows of knots seemed crazy.

Lindri examined the band of lace, her grey eyes sharp. 'Perhaps I am.' She shrugged. 'Perhaps not.'

One of the smallest children in the village, blonde Krista, was inching closer. She stared at Lindri and at me, her finger in her half-open mouth. Lindri smiled at Krista, speaking before I could warn her about the child.

'Hello, young one. Can I do something for you?'

Krista turned to run—she was shy to the point of sickness, even with most of the people in our village. Then she stumbled and fell with a cry. I ran to pick her up—she was fond of me—and I had to bite my lip to keep from crying out. She had cut her palm on a rock in the street; I could see the bones of her hand under the deep, ugly gash. She was screaming in pain and fright.

'Hush, hush.' Lindri took Krista from me, brushing her off with an efficient hand. 'So much noise. Let me see.'

To my surprise, Krista held the bleeding hand up for Lindri to look at. Already blood dripped onto the ground from the cut, and I shook my head. Such a wound meant days of wearing a bandage, the risk of infection was terrible. If things went badly, pretty Krista would lose her hand.

'Nonsense,' Lindri was telling Krista. She took the little one over to the cart, holding Krista's hand beneath the spout of her water-barrel as she rinsed the wound clean. She whisked a strip of white cloth from the piles on the tray and sat on a stool, never letting Krista get free. I was surprised the child wasn't struggling in the stranger's hold—only her mother, her father and I could touch her at all.

Lindri bandaged her hand quickly and neatly, talking to Krista as she worked. She finished by tying the loose ends into an oddly-shaped knot directly over the wound, tapping the knot lightly with her fingers when she was done. 'All fixed,' she told Krista. 'Keep it clean, mind. I think you'll see when you take the bandage off that you aren't hurt as badly as you thought.'

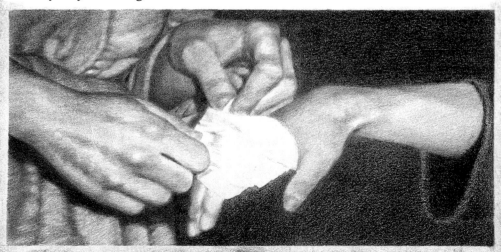

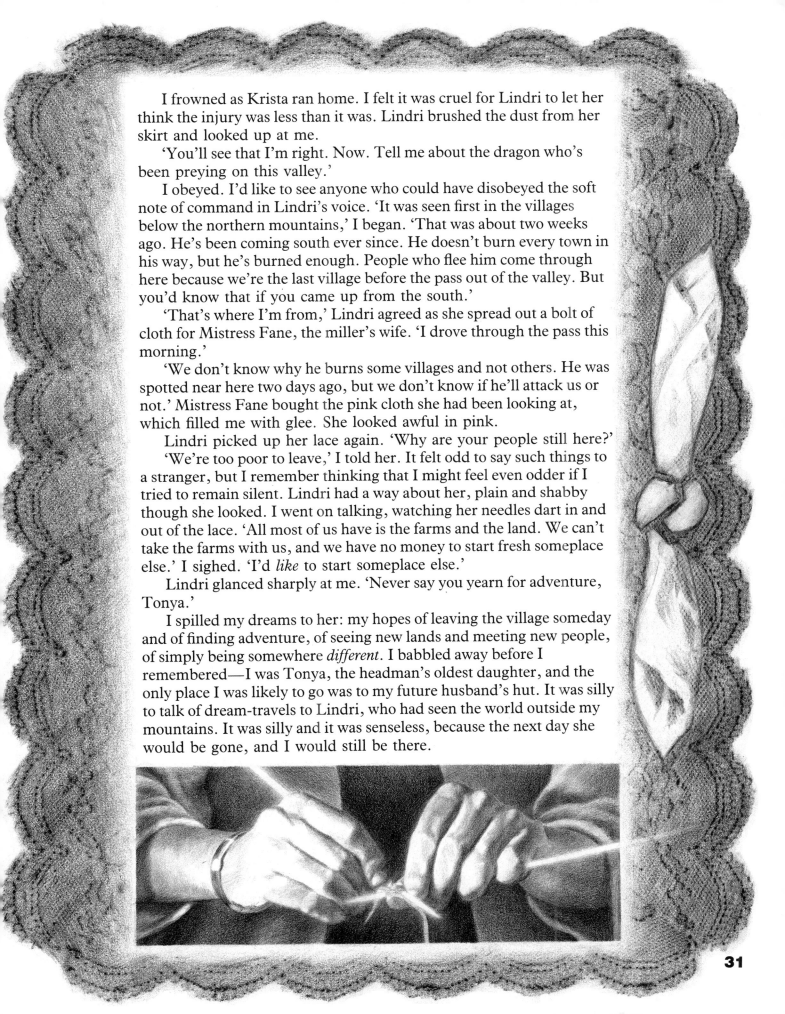

I frowned as Krista ran home. I felt it was cruel for Lindri to let her think the injury was less than it was. Lindri brushed the dust from her skirt and looked up at me.

'You'll see that I'm right. Now. Tell me about the dragon who's been preying on this valley.'

I obeyed. I'd like to see anyone who could have disobeyed the soft note of command in Lindri's voice. 'It was seen first in the villages below the northern mountains,' I began. 'That was about two weeks ago. He's been coming south ever since. He doesn't burn every town in his way, but he's burned enough. People who flee him come through here because we're the last village before the pass out of the valley. But you'd know that if you came up from the south.'

'That's where I'm from,' Lindri agreed as she spread out a bolt of cloth for Mistress Fane, the miller's wife. 'I drove through the pass this morning.'

'We don't know why he burns some villages and not others. He was spotted near here two days ago, but we don't know if he'll attack us or not.' Mistress Fane bought the pink cloth she had been looking at, which filled me with glee. She looked awful in pink.

Lindri picked up her lace again. 'Why are your people still here?'

'We're too poor to leave,' I told her. It felt odd to say such things to a stranger, but I remember thinking that I might feel even odder if I tried to remain silent. Lindri had a way about her, plain and shabby though she looked. I went on talking, watching her needles dart in and out of the lace. 'All most of us has is the farms and the land. We can't take the farms with us, and we have no money to start fresh someplace else.' I sighed. 'I'd *like* to start someplace else.'

Lindri glanced sharply at me. 'Never say you yearn for adventure, Tonya.'

I spilled my dreams to her: my hopes of leaving the village someday and of finding adventure, of seeing new lands and meeting new people, of simply being somewhere *different*. I babbled away before I remembered—I was Tonya, the headman's oldest daughter, and the only place I was likely to go was to my future husband's hut. It was silly to talk of dream-travels to Lindri, who had seen the world outside my mountains. It was silly and it was senseless, because the next day she would be gone, and I would still be there.

'Where are you going now?' I asked.

She looked at the sun, which was heading down the western half of the sky, and exchanged her lace for knitting. 'North,' she replied briefly. 'Into the mountains.'

'You can't go there!'

Her grey eyes were amused as she looked at me. 'Why not?'

'You could get hurt,' I told her. 'Wild animals live in those mountains—dragons, and bears taller than a tall man, so I've been told, and giant cats—'

Lindri shrugged. 'I like animals. None of them kill without a reason.'

I was about to argue with her when Riv interrupted us. It was turning late, and he was just in with his flock. 'Excuse me,' he said politely, picking up a small square of folded lace. 'I want to know how much this is.'

There was no expression on Lindri's face as she looked at him. 'Two minims.'

'For just this little bit?' Riv asked, looking at the lace. It was beautiful, filmy white stuff, and I was willing to bet the price Lindri had given him was less than what she could get for it anywhere else. He handed it to her. 'Hold this, please. I want to look at the rest.' He went to the other end of the tray while I scowled at his back.

'Tell me about him,' Lindri commanded me.

I took a deep breath to keep from yelling that it wasn't fair. 'He's getting married next month,' I whispered, keeping an eye on Riv. 'His girl Aura is my best friend. She's standing over there, the one with the basket on her arm. Riv's chief of the shepherds, but he hasn't been chief through a spring shearing, so he hasn't any money. And all Aura ever wanted was a lace veil, like the great ladies have in the cities.' I noticed Lindri was tugging on the edges of the lace Riv had given her, and I frowned. I thought she might be getting it dirty. 'No one else here had a lace veil, so they say Aura thinks she's better than the rest of us. But that isn't true! She's my best friend—wouldn't *I* know? She just wants something pretty, that's all. And people act—'

'Hush,' Lindri said. She looked at Riv, who was coming back. 'See anything you'd rather have?'

Riv was holding out two copper minims. His face was beet-coloured with shame. 'No. This will do.' He was trying to smile, but he wasn't succeeding. 'It isn't a whole veil, but—well, it's very pretty,' he finished.

Lindri pocketed the coppers and handed Riv the folded square. I blinked. Boys were putting out torches, it had gotten so dark, but I still would have sworn the square of lace was bulkier than it had been when Riv put in it Lindri's hands. 'Enjoy it,' the peddler-woman told Riv, smiling. 'And may your marriage be happy.'

I watched as Riv walked over to Aura, the lace behind his back. 'It's just not fair,' I muttered.

Riv was talking to Aura, and then holding out the lace, 'What's not fair?' Lindri asked.

'Old, ugly people like Miller Fane and his wife have nice things they don't enjoy, but Aura and Riv—'

I gasped. Riv was holding the lace above his head as length after length of it spilled from his hands, shimmering white in the torch-light. He had to raise his hands higher and higher to keep it from touching the ground, while Aura laughed and cried at the same time.

'How did that happen?' I whispered.

Aura and Riv tried to make Lindri take it back, but she seemed as surprised as they were. 'That's the bit you paid for,' she finally told them firmly. 'Ask Tonya if it ever left my hands after you gave it to me.'

And that was the biggest puzzle of all, because I had been talking to her—and watching her—the whole time, and the only thing she did with that piece of lace was tug on it. I *knew* it had been a square of one or two thicknesses when Riv handed it to Lindri, but I couldn't prove it. They went away at last, Aura crying on Riv's shoulder as he carefully re-folded the lace.

Lindri shook her head, straightening the goods on her tray. 'People should inspect what they buy carefully, Tonya,' she said wisely. 'They never know what they've purchased, otherwise.'

I was about to ask her what Riv *had* bought when my father—the headman—came to greet Lindri, accompanied by the other two elders—Priest Rand and Wizard Kenby. The priest was saying polite things to her when the wizard started looking at her wares. Suddenly he picked up a square of linen and held it to the light, scowling slightly. 'There is something strange about this piece,' he began.

Lindri took it from him. 'Don't touch unless you plan to buy,' she snapped. I looked at her with surprise—she had been so pleasant all afternoon that I hadn't thought she could sound so nasty. Wizard Kenby's eyes narrowed and he opened his mouth to speak, but we were all distracted when my brother Selm galloped into the square. Normally

Selm was calm and slow-going, but when he reined up before our father, he was in as much of a lather as his horse.

'I saw it settling on Tower Rock!' he gasped. 'Long and green, like we were told! And it was flaming!'

People quickly arrived in the square until all of us stood in the torchlight, worrying about the dragon. Even I felt scared. The worst of it was not knowing at all what the dragon might do. Whatever we decided, we were gambling, with our farms and with our lives. By the time Krista arrived with her parents, everyone was quiet, waiting to hear what my father, the priest and the wizard decided. Miller Fane and his wife arrived with their horse-drawn cart—the only one in the village—piled high with their things. They could afford to run, but what of the rest of us?

Wizard Kenby was saying 'I believe there *is* a way . . .' when Krista's mother saw the bandage on her girl's hand was dirty and bedraggled. I watched her tugging at the strange knot while we waited to hear Kenby out.

'Tell us all,' Tanner Cly yelled to the wizard. Krista's mother gave up on trying to undo the knot and cut it with her belt knife.

'I have been trying to remember the various remedies for a plague of dragons,' Kenby said loudly. His squeaky voice quavered with the effort. 'A spear made of silver, of course, wielded by a virtuous man—'

Someone called, 'If there was enough silver here to make a spear, Wizard, you'd have had it all by now.'

My father scowled. 'The wizard is trying to aid us,' he said heavily. 'Listen to him.'

Kenby looked smug for a moment and waited for us to hush once more. 'A dragon may also be lured to his death in a pit of fire, or buried in a river of ice.' He tugged his nose for a moment. 'But there is another way to placate a dragon, and I have remembered it at last.'

'Is it as impossible as the others?' Miller Fane wanted to know. 'There are no pits of fire or rivers of ice in the valley, and we are running out of time!'

People muttered agreement, and Kenby raised his voice. 'It is not as impossible as those others, but it is costly. You may think it better to abandon your homes.'

'Where will we go?' Krista's mother cried. She stopped unwinding the bandage from her daughter's palm. 'We have lived here for generations!'

Everyone shouted their agreement.

'You must give the dragon something,' Kenby said, raising his thin voice so he could be heard. 'Something to assuage his hunger.'

'Oh, no,' Lindri whispered tiredly.

I missed Kenby's next words because I was staring at Krista. Her mother had the bandage off at last. She was turning the little one's palm back and forth in the light, trying to see where it had been cut. So was I. There was no sign of the ugly gash that had marred Krista's hand when Lindri put the bandage on.

'. . . a young girl,' I heard Kenby say. 'Unmarried. A virgin.'

Everyone was silent. To offer the beast one of our own . . . A woman began to cry.

'You must draw lots,' Kenby went on. 'You must be fair.'

'Drivel.' Everyone stared at Lindri, who stood beside her cart. She looked at Kenby scornfully. 'Absolute nonsense. Do you seriously think a dragon can taste the difference between a virgin and a wizard, old man?'

'You are a stranger here,' Miller Fane called to her. 'Speak to our wizard with respect.'

'Your wizard does not know what he's talking about.' Lindri's voice was calm and clear. 'Dragons hate the taste of human flesh.'

'Legend is filled with the sacrifices made to dragons!' Kenby was turning red. Just when he had everyone's attention and respect, this peddler-woman in her dusty dress and boots was trying to make him look like a fool.

'Of course a dragon will eat a human if a human is staked out like a goat,' Lindri admitted. 'They are not very smart. This one will eat your virgin, and then he will be sick. Did you know a dragon flames only when he is ill? He will pass over *your* homes before he realizes what has happened—but he will burn the next village he sees to the ground. You will have killed a girl needlessly, and you will have caused others to lose their homes. All for the lack of a little sense on your part, *wizard.*'

My father was dark with anger. 'You have said more than enough,' he told Lindri. 'You are a guest here, and Kenby is our wizard. Be silent, or our young men will see you on your way.'

Lindri examined my father for a moment, as if she could see through his face into his head. I was angry and ashamed. *I* knew my father's failings, but he was my father. What right did a stranger have to look at him as if he was a fool?

Lindri shrugged and sat down. My father looked at us, waiting for another sign of rebellion, then turned to Kenby. 'How young must they be?'

The wizard swelled with pride. Lindri had been silenced, and now everyone waited for him to tell us what to do. He took his time. 'They must be of marriageable age, and no younger than twelve,' he said at last.

There were seven girls—as I have said, the village was very small. Some of my friends were already married: I could see them clinging to their husbands. We seven were separated from the others, and Carpenter Lykam cut a rod into a short piece and six longer ones. The wizard made a bag out of my mother's shawl, and the pieces were dumped inside. The priest said a prayer over the bag. Then we were told to each step up and take a piece of wood without looking. Lindri was silent, knitting busily, her eyes as calm as if we were play-acting for her entertainment.

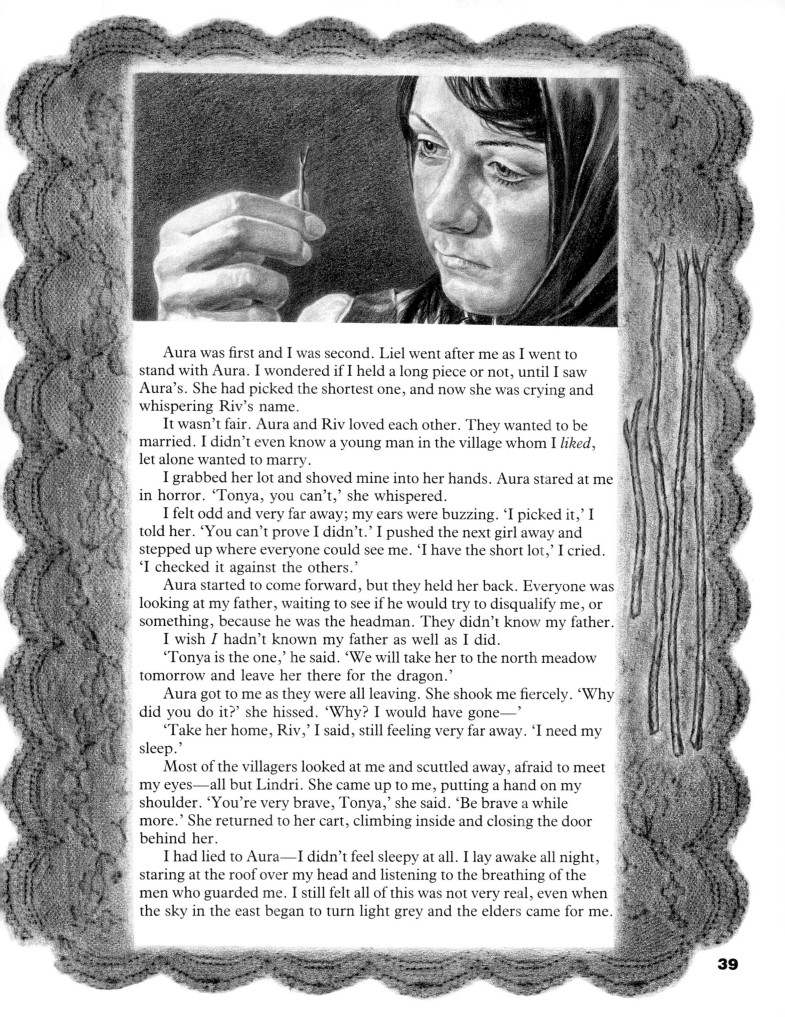

Aura was first and I was second. Liel went after me as I went to stand with Aura. I wondered if I held a long piece or not, until I saw Aura's. She had picked the shortest one, and now she was crying and whispering Riv's name.

It wasn't fair. Aura and Riv loved each other. They wanted to be married. I didn't even know a young man in the village whom I *liked*, let alone wanted to marry.

I grabbed her lot and shoved mine into her hands. Aura stared at me in horror. 'Tonya, you can't,' she whispered.

I felt odd and very far away; my ears were buzzing. 'I picked it,' I told her. 'You can't prove I didn't.' I pushed the next girl away and stepped up where everyone could see me. 'I have the short lot,' I cried. 'I checked it against the others.'

Aura started to come forward, but they held her back. Everyone was looking at my father, waiting to see if he would try to disqualify me, or something, because he was the headman. They didn't know my father.

I wish *I* hadn't known my father as well as I did.

'Tonya is the one,' he said. 'We will take her to the north meadow tomorrow and leave her there for the dragon.'

Aura got to me as they were all leaving. She shook me fiercely. 'Why did you do it?' she hissed. 'Why? I would have gone—'

'Take her home, Riv,' I said, still feeling very far away. 'I need my sleep.'

Most of the villagers looked at me and scuttled away, afraid to meet my eyes—all but Lindri. She came up to me, putting a hand on my shoulder. 'You're very brave, Tonya,' she said. 'Be brave a while more.' She returned to her cart, climbing inside and closing the door behind her.

I had lied to Aura—I didn't feel sleepy at all. I lay awake all night, staring at the roof over my head and listening to the breathing of the men who guarded me. I still felt all of this was not very real, even when the sky in the east began to turn light grey and the elders came for me.

The post was already standing in the middle of the large northern meadow, brand-new chains hanging from it. The priest locked the shackles around my hands, muttering a prayer as he kept an eye on the distant Tower Rock. Just a touch of sun showed over the horizon when they left me, running to hide in the woods at the meadow's edge. I was alone, facing the Tower Rock and the humped form that sat on top of it.

Once he begins to fly, I thought, *it won't be too long before he's here. It'll be over before I can feel it.* At least, I hoped so.

I was standing there, waiting, when I heard a horse's harness jingle. Lindri stopped her cart a little way from me and her piebald gelding put his head down to graze. The elders were yelling—they must have been telling her to get away from me—but they were too afraid to leave the protection of the trees.

Lindri was wearing a clean blue dress, and she had wiped yesterday's dust off her high boots. She looked as fresh and awake as if she had been up for hours. She glanced at the Tower Rock, where the dragon was unfurling his wings, and gathered my shackles up in her hands.

'This comedy has gone far enough,' she said, looking the chains over, 'although I'm sure you don't think so.' She tapped each lock with her fingers—just as she had tapped Krista's bandage—and the shackles sprang open. She pulled a short piece of twine from her skirt-pocket. 'Get out of here, Tonya. I'll wait for the dragon.'

Suddenly I felt wide awake and alert. I didn't go far—I went to her cart and waited, stroking the piebald's nose and ignoring the cries of the elders, just as she did. She faced north as calmly as she had stood in the square. Only her fingers moved, tying multitudes of knots in her piece of twine.

I stared. The clumps of knots were growing far more than the length of her string was responsible for, spilling from her working hands down to the ground. The dragon was just leaping into the air from the Tower Rock when she grabbed the masses of knots, gathering them back into her hands until they formed a huge bundle.

I sneaked a look at Wizard Kenby. He was screaming and jumping in a fury. My father was shaking him, and the priest was muttering prayers.

The dragon soared in low over the meadow, little bits of flame streaking from his open jaws. Lindri waited until he was overhead. Swiftly she crouched, then leaped, hurling the mass of knots into the air. Like a living thing the net wrapped itself around the dragon, wings, snout, claws and all. The great lizard spouted flame and screeched with alarm as he dropped to the ground, landing with a thump in the meadow. He flamed once more, helplessly, but the net didn't catch fire.

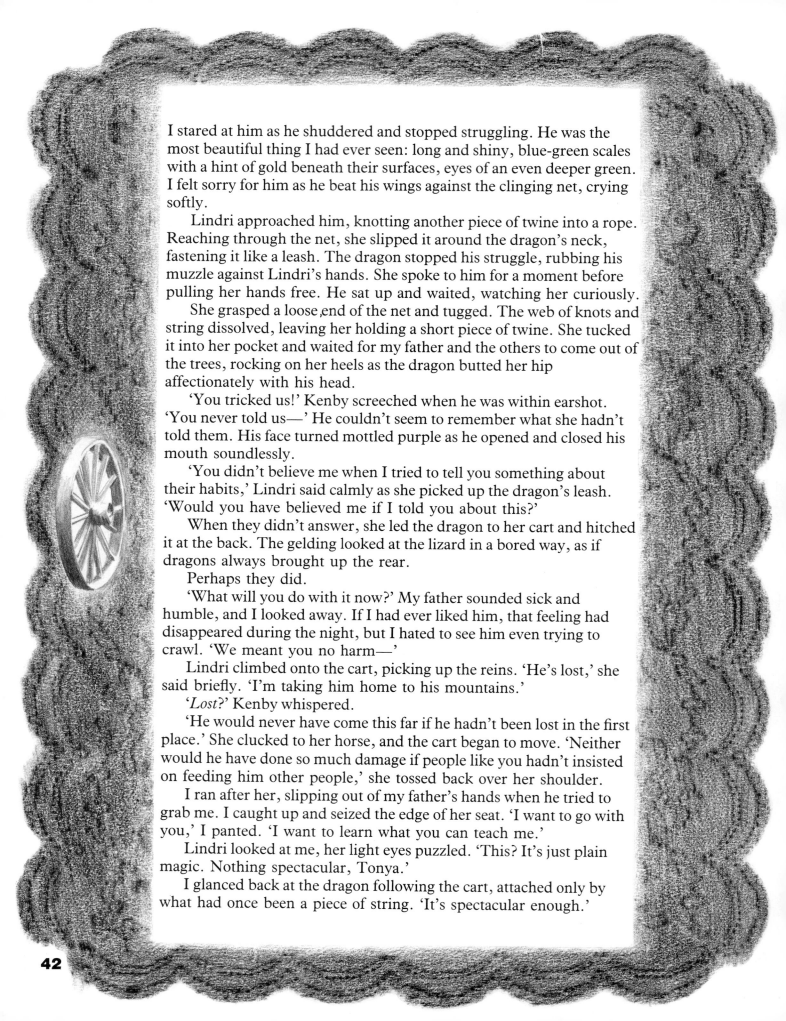

I stared at him as he shuddered and stopped struggling. He was the most beautiful thing I had ever seen: long and shiny, blue-green scales with a hint of gold beneath their surfaces, eyes of an even deeper green. I felt sorry for him as he beat his wings against the clinging net, crying softly.

Lindri approached him, knotting another piece of twine into a rope. Reaching through the net, she slipped it around the dragon's neck, fastening it like a leash. The dragon stopped his struggle, rubbing his muzzle against Lindri's hands. She spoke to him for a moment before pulling her hands free. He sat up and waited, watching her curiously.

She grasped a loose end of the net and tugged. The web of knots and string dissolved, leaving her holding a short piece of twine. She tucked it into her pocket and waited for my father and the others to come out of the trees, rocking on her heels as the dragon butted her hip affectionately with his head.

'You tricked us!' Kenby screeched when he was within earshot. 'You never told us—' He couldn't seem to remember what she hadn't told them. His face turned mottled purple as he opened and closed his mouth soundlessly.

'You didn't believe me when I tried to tell you something about their habits,' Lindri said calmly as she picked up the dragon's leash. 'Would you have believed me if I told you about this?'

When they didn't answer, she led the dragon to her cart and hitched it at the back. The gelding looked at the lizard in a bored way, as if dragons always brought up the rear.

Perhaps they did.

'What will you do with it now?' My father sounded sick and humble, and I looked away. If I had ever liked him, that feeling had disappeared during the night, but I hated to see him even trying to crawl. 'We meant you no harm—'

Lindri climbed onto the cart, picking up the reins. 'He's lost,' she said briefly. 'I'm taking him home to his mountains.'

'*Lost?*' Kenby whispered.

'He would never have come this far if he hadn't been lost in the first place.' She clucked to her horse, and the cart began to move. 'Neither would he have done so much damage if people like you hadn't insisted on feeding him other people,' she tossed back over her shoulder.

I ran after her, slipping out of my father's hands when he tried to grab me. I caught up and seized the edge of her seat. 'I want to go with you,' I panted. 'I want to learn what you can teach me.'

Lindri looked at me, her light eyes puzzled. 'This? It's just plain magic. Nothing spectacular, Tonya.'

I glanced back at the dragon following the cart, attached only by what had once been a piece of string. 'It's spectacular enough.'

Lindri laughed, and I realized she wasn't old at all—that she had just a couple of years more than I did. 'Come up, then,' she said, offering her hand. 'What I have to teach you, I will.'

'Plain magic,' she calls it. Hah!

3 Deadly Filaments

'There's more bad news,' Russell said gloomily to Mizzo. 'Our ship was able to identify the intruder. It's Ekridolak.'

Mizzo's small hands clenched. 'That vicious heap of black hair . . . He *would* be the first.'

'And the Gathering sent us a message,' Russell went on. 'It seems that Ekridolak has already visited a world much like this one, in a star system not far away. And the first thing he did was—to kill the Sentinel.'

'So he seeks to do the same here,' Mizzo said, his voice even sharper with the realization. 'To come after us.'

Before Russell could reply, Lindy broke in, tremulously. 'Who is this alien you're talking about?'

Russell looked at her as if surprised to see the children still there. 'Ekridolak,' he told her, 'is a professional thief and assassin. He is a master of weapons, ruthless and single-minded, not caring who or what he hurts to get what he wants. He has done terrible damage on many other worlds, and has always escaped the peace forces of those worlds.'

'Couldn't you get some of them to come after him?' Jeff asked.

Mizzo laughed sharply. 'A fine thing, a detachment of alien police charging around Earth. They would do as much damage as Ekridolak. Nor could they catch him.'

'No one has ever caught him,' Russell added. 'He's a *shape shifter*, like many of the creatures on his planet. It's an automatic protection. The moment he feels in danger, whatever world he's on, he changes instantly into the shape of some harmless creature of that world. And so he gets away.'

'What can you do?' Lindy asked, looking shaken.

Russell shrugged. 'The only thing we can do. Wait for him to come after us. And try to stay alive long enough to find a way to trap him, or to drive him away from Earth.' He smiled grimly. 'We can't attack or kill him—but we can certainly *defend* ourselves, when he tries to kill us. We'll think of something.'

'And there are two of us,' Mizzo put in, 'while he is alone.'

'But you two had better leave now,' Russell went on. 'Some unpleasant things could be happening around here soon. You won't be in any danger as long as you stay well away from this house.'

The children nodded mutely, and moved towards the door. Then Lindy glanced back with anxious eyes. 'I hope you think of a way to stop him, Russ,' she said.

'And I wish we could help,' Jeff added.

Russell smiled. 'Don't worry. And you *can* help—by staying out of the way, and by keeping your promise. It's absolutely necessary that you never reveal our secret to anyone—*whatever* happens.'

'We won't,' Jeff said solemnly.

'We swear it,' Lindy whispered.

And then they slipped out of the house, back into the peaceful, ordinary, small-town Sunday morning.

The children wandered slowly along the street, in silence, their minds whirling with all the strange and disturbing things that they had learned that morning. In that short while it seemed that their entire world had been thrown off-balance, and it was all nearly too much to grasp. Yet their dazed minds could not stop thinking about the most important facts—that they had met two friendly aliens who were protectors of Earth, and that a 'heap of black hair' who was a vicious alien criminal was seeking to destroy them.

'We *have* to help them,' Lindy said suddenly, her voice low and intense.

'How?' Jeff demanded. 'What can *we* do against some alien killer who can do all the things that Russ said?'

'I don't know,' Lindy said miserably. 'But we can't just stay at home and let them be killed . . .'

She broke off with a gasp. From behind a clump of forsythia in a nearby garden, a large, dark, shaggy form had appeared, leaping towards them.

But the form also had a long feathery tail, wagging vigorously, and a pink tongue hanging foolishly out of its mouth—with which it tried to lick Jeff's face as it jumped joyfully up on him.

'Mutt!' Jeff said. 'Get down!'

Lindy sneezed. Then she sneezed again, and again. 'Ged hib do go hobe,' she said to Jeff pleadingly, in the voice of someone with a streaming cold.

'Home, Mutt!' Jeff said at once, sternly. 'Go on! Get home!' The dog's head and tail drooped, but he wandered obediently off. 'Sorry,' Jeff said to Lindy.

She sniffed, wiped her nose, and smiled wanly. 'It's not your fault I'm allergic to animals,' she said, her voice nearly normal again. 'Not Mutt's fault, either.'

'Wish we could have pets like Mizzo,' Jeff said. 'You weren't allergic to *him*.'

'No,' Lindy said wistfully. Suddenly her eyes were bright with tears. 'Jeff, do you think—they'll be all right?'

''Course,' Jeff said stoutly. 'They've been Sentinels before—Russ said. This Ekrido . . . whatsit . . . won't beat him and Mizzo.'

'I hope not,' Lindy said as they drifted away towards their homes, across the street from Russell Carron's little house. 'But I still wish there was some way we could help . . .'

Many hours later, after darkness had fallen over that quiet street, Russell appeared as if by magic in the deep shadows of his back garden.

He had paid a brief visit to his spaceship, where it was invisibly orbiting the Earth at a distance far beyond any human satellites. The ship was equipped with a device known as a Transplacer beam, and Russell had summoned it after dark, when the ship was in the right place overhead.

The beam had reached down from space to surround him with the faint haze of an almost invisible force field. Then, unseen and fully protected by that field, he had been whisked upwards by the beam, into his ship.

It had been a risk, he knew, leaving Mizzo alone in the house. But he was expecting the killer, Ekridolak, to wait a while—to look around, make his plans—before launching an attack. And it was a risk that had to be taken, for Russell needed some special equipment from his ship.

As he had told the children, though he and Mizzo could not commit violence or take a life, they were very much able to *defend* themselves. They were certainly not going to sit around waiting for Ekridolak without being fully prepared.

So, when the Transplacer beam set Russell quietly down in the darkness of his back garden, he was carrying a container of strange, miniaturized objects. The force field disappeared, so that he seemed to materialize out of nothing. For a moment he stood still, looking around at the darkness, listening hard, making sure that his magical reappearance had not been seen by other eyes. But all was well. He seemed entirely alone and unwatched, among the shadows.

Until one of the shadows themselves moved, through the air above his head.

He tensed, his heart lurching, staring up at the night sky. It had just been a flicker of movement, seen at the corner of his eye. And there might have been the faintest sound of quiet, sweeping wings. Some night bird, then—perhaps an owl.

But he had never seen or heard any owls around that part of town, before.

Still tense and watchful, he moved towards the house, and slipped in through the back door. All was silent and in darkness, as he had left it, for Mizzo could see fairly well in the dark. But the little alien was probably upstairs, asleep, Russell thought. He set his container down in the kitchen, and went quietly into the main living room, straining his eyes to try to see something in the almost solid blackness.

He stepped carefully past the places where he knew—though he could not see—that the furniture stood. Then his heart lurched again as his foot struck against something that should not have been there. But at once he heard the slight sloshing sound, and realized. It was the bucket of water that he had used to wash the car. He had been so involved with the children, and then with the dire message from his AID, that he had forgotten to take the bucket into the kitchen to empty it.

I'm a poor housekeeper, he thought wryly, as he stepped around the bucket. Then he had reached the heavy table, and switched on the small lamp that stood upon it.

And every fibre of his body seemed to turn to ice, with sudden fear, as he became aware of two things.

First, Mizzo was sprawled on the floor, limp, eyes closed, looking entirely lifeless.

Secondly, he had heard a faint, extremely high-pitched musical sound—as if someone had delicately stroked a guitar string tuned almost beyond human hearing.

The sound continued, faint, sweet and absolutely deadly. Russell had heard that sound before, and knew what it meant.

It was made by an alien invention known as 'Krastian filaments'—like long, stiff wires that were no more than two or three *atoms* thick. The filaments were in the room, being activated by his presence, by the heat of his body. Soon there would be many of them, swinging invisibly back and forth like pendulums, sweeping through the room.

And there was no substance in the galaxy that a Krastian filament could not slice through, like a cheese wire through soft butter.

IF YOU WERE THE SENTINEL, EMPTY-HANDED IN A ROOM FULL OF DEADLINESS, COULD YOU THINK OF A WAY TO SAVE YOURSELF? THE STORY CONTINUES ON PAGE 74.

Can *you* SURVive on an aL/éN PlaneT ?

5 SUDDENLY AN INSECT-LIKE CREATURE DROPS FROM ONE OF THE 'TREES' AND HANGS IN FRONT OF YOUR FACE. YOU DO NOT RECOGNIZE IT. IT WAS NOT MENTIONED IN THE ALIEN LIFE FORM DATA.

WILL YOU BRUSH PAST IT INTO THE GLADE?   (A)

WILL YOU STOP AND EXAMINE IT?   (B)

WILL YOU SLASH AT THE CREATURE'S LIFELINE WITH A KNIFE?   (C)

6 HOW WILL YOU GET PAST THE BEAST WITH TWO MOUTHS?

WILL YOU TIPTOE PAST BEFORE THE BEAST SEES YOU?   (A)

WILL YOU IGNORE THE BEAST AND REST IN THE GLADE?   (B)

WILL YOU PICK ONE OF THE RED FRUIT AND OFFER IT TO THE BEAST TO EAT?   (C)

The GLADE .....

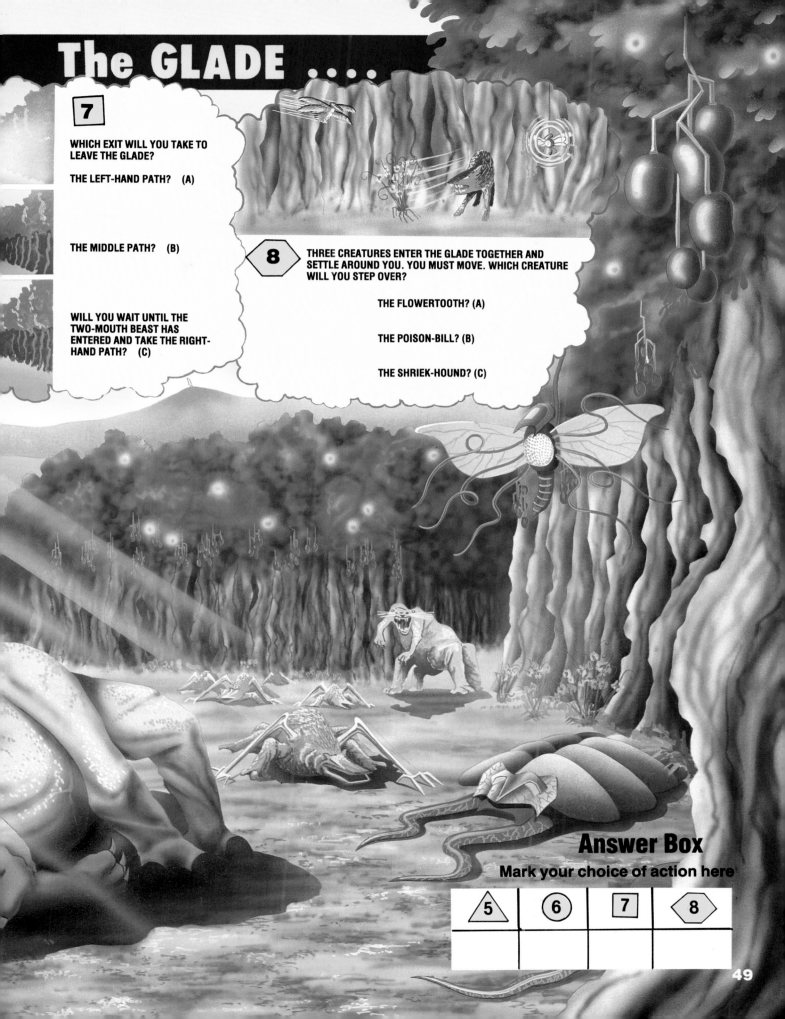

7

WHICH EXIT WILL YOU TAKE TO
LEAVE THE GLADE?

THE LEFT-HAND PATH?   (A)

THE MIDDLE PATH?   (B)

WILL YOU WAIT UNTIL THE
TWO-MOUTH BEAST HAS
ENTERED AND TAKE THE RIGHT-
HAND PATH?   (C)

8

THREE CREATURES ENTER THE GLADE TOGETHER AND
SETTLE AROUND YOU. YOU MUST MOVE. WHICH CREATURE
WILL YOU STEP OVER?

THE FLOWERTOOTH? (A)

THE POISON-BILL? (B)

THE SHRIEK-HOUND? (C)

Answer Box

Mark your choice of action here

5	6	7	8

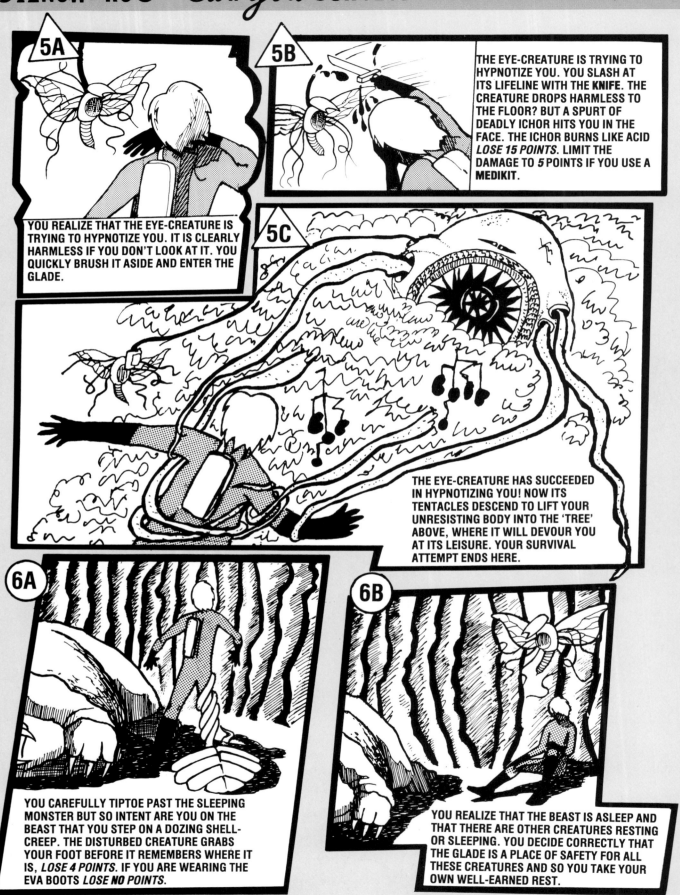

5A YOU REALIZE THAT THE EYE-CREATURE IS TRYING TO HYPNOTIZE YOU. IT IS CLEARLY HARMLESS IF YOU DON'T LOOK AT IT. YOU QUICKLY BRUSH IT ASIDE AND ENTER THE GLADE.

5B THE EYE-CREATURE IS TRYING TO HYPNOTIZE YOU. YOU SLASH AT ITS LIFELINE WITH THE **KNIFE**. THE CREATURE DROPS HARMLESS TO THE FLOOR? BUT A SPURT OF DEADLY ICHOR HITS YOU IN THE FACE. THE ICHOR BURNS LIKE ACID *LOSE 15 POINTS*. LIMIT THE DAMAGE TO *5* POINTS IF YOU USE A MEDIKIT.

5C THE EYE-CREATURE HAS SUCCEEDED IN HYPNOTIZING YOU! NOW ITS TENTACLES DESCEND TO LIFT YOUR UNRESISTING BODY INTO THE 'TREE' ABOVE, WHERE IT WILL DEVOUR YOU AT ITS LEISURE. YOUR SURVIVAL ATTEMPT ENDS HERE.

6A YOU CAREFULLY TIPTOE PAST THE SLEEPING MONSTER BUT SO INTENT ARE YOU ON THE BEAST THAT YOU STEP ON A DOZING SHELL-CREEP. THE DISTURBED CREATURE GRABS YOUR FOOT BEFORE IT REMEMBERS WHERE IT IS, *LOSE 4 POINTS*. IF YOU ARE WEARING THE EVA BOOTS *LOSE **NO** POINTS*.

6B YOU REALIZE THAT THE BEAST IS ASLEEP AND THAT THERE ARE OTHER CREATURES RESTING OR SLEEPING. YOU DECIDE CORRECTLY THAT THE GLADE IS A PLACE OF SAFETY FOR ALL THESE CREATURES AND SO YOU TAKE YOUR OWN WELL-EARNED REST.

6C

THE TWO-MOUTHED BEAST DOES NOT TAKE KINDLY TO BEING ROUSED FROM ITS RARE MOMENTS OF REST BY AN IDIOT WAVING THE TASTELESS GORMFRUIT IN ITS FACE. ANYBODY SHOULD BE ABLE TO SEE THAT IT ONLY EATS MEAT WITH TEETH LIKE THAT. THE BEAST SWIPES AT YOU WITH ONE OF ITS HEAVY FORE-CLAWS. YOU ARE LUCKY, THE BEAST IS ONLY HALF-AWAKE AND THE BLOW IS GLANCING, *LOSE 13 LIFEPOINTS*. A FULLY AWAKE BEAST WOULD HAVE KILLED YOU IN ONE BLOW. BUT NOW THE BEAST SUBSIDES BACK TO ITS SLUMBER.

7A

YOU TAKE THE LEFT PATH AND IMMEDIATELY REALIZE YOU HAVE MADE AN ERROR. THIS PATH IS AN ILLUSION. THE TREES HERE USE STRANGE MENTAL POWERS TO CATCH FOREST CREATURES. LUCKILY YOU ARE INTELLIGENT ENOUGH TO RESIST, BUT YOU FEEL DRAINED. *LOSE 7 POINTS.*

7B

THIS PATH LOOKS A LOT SAFE THAN THE OTHER TWO. YOU ARE RIGHT—IT OFFERS NO PARTICULAR DANGER AND YOU CONTINUE ON YOUR WAY THROUGH THE ALIEN FOREST.

7C

YOU CAUTIOUSLY WAIT UNTIL THE TWO-MOUTH BEAST HAS ENTERED THE GLADE BUT UNLUCKILY FOR YOU THIS IS A PATH BY WHICH THE FOREST CREATURES ENTER THE GLADE. YOU ARE SOON MET BY ANOTHER TWO-MOUTH BEAST. IF YOU HAVE A LASER YOU MANAGE TO FIRE AT IT AND WOUND THE CREATURE ENOUGH TO GET YOURSELF AWAY WITH A LEG INJURY— *LOSE 12 SURVIVAL POINTS*. IF YOU DON'T HAVE A LASER THEN YOU QUICKLY FIND YOURSELF BEING DIGESTED BY THE BEAST'S SECOND MOUTH AND YOUR SURVIVAL ATTEMPT ENDS HERE.

8B

THE POISON-BILL SQUIRTS A JET OF ACID AT YOU FOR DISTURBING ITS ROOST. *LOSE 8 POINTS* OR USE A MEDIKIT.

8A

AS YOU STEP OVER THE FLOWERTOOTH IT TAKES A LARGE BITE OUT OF YOUR DELICIOUS LEG. *LOSE 9 POINTS* OR USE A MEDIKIT.

8C YOU STEP QUITE SAFELY OVER THE SHRIEK-HOUND. IT ISN'T HUNGRY AS IT FEEDS BY NIGHT.

KRAIL'S WORLD

by David Garnett

APE CAPSULE... TIME TO LAUNCH 30 SEC.

COMPUTER MALFUNCTION

DISTANCE: 2632 KM
LANDING COORDINATES:
19 S 45W
S2
S1
N
POSITION
TRAJECTORY
S

The sky was aglow with thousands and thousands of stars.

Krail was staring at them through the periscope above the pilot's seat as the moon came up, and in the dim light he was at last able to take a proper look at the area where he had landed. It was worse than he feared, but he supposed it didn't make much difference because he wasn't going anywhere. He was trapped here.

A few minutes later the second moon rose, a huge pale orange disc which lit up the bleak landscape even more.

53

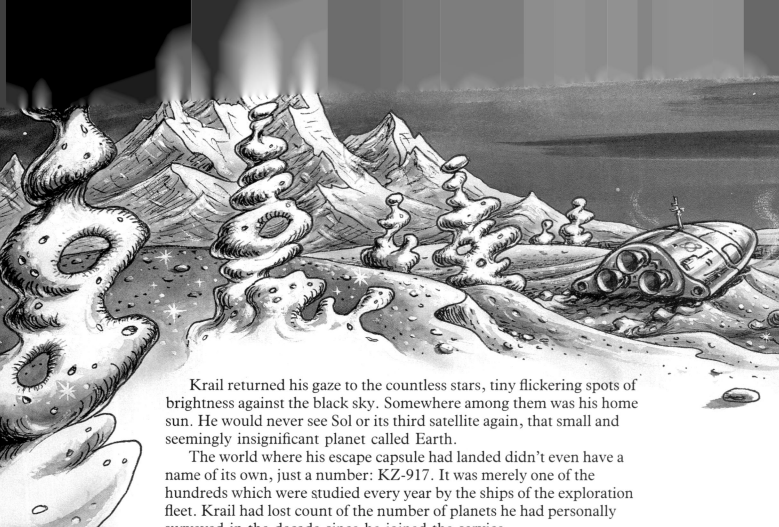

Krail returned his gaze to the countless stars, tiny flickering spots of brightness against the black sky. Somewhere among them was his home sun. He would never see Sol or its third satellite again, that small and seemingly insignificant planet called Earth.

The world where his escape capsule had landed didn't even have a name of its own, just a number: KZ-917. It was merely one of the hundreds which were studied every year by the ships of the exploration fleet. Krail had lost count of the number of planets he had personally surveyed in the decade since he joined the service.

Not every star had planets of its own. But even if only one in a thousand did, that still left millions of worlds to be investigated. It was a task which would never be completed, because planets were being discovered faster than they could be surveyed.

The vast majority of these were totally unsuited to any form of life, ranging from desolate worlds where the temperature never rose above absolute zero to blazing infernos. There was no need to check such hostile environments, but for every ten thousand impossible planets, there was one which could perhaps support human life—worlds where the gravity and climate and atmosphere were similar to that of Earth itself.

Scores of exploration ships hunted through the galaxy for such planets. Their primary mission was to discover worlds where humans could live, but they were also searching for signs of life—any kind of life. When mankind had originally burst out from the confines of his own solar system a century ago, people had been convinced that there must have been other worlds where life had developed. Not necessarily advanced life, perhaps only some primitive vegetation on a far-off world circling an unknown star.

But after a hundred year quest, nothing had been discovered, nothing at all. The more time which passed and the farther that humanity probed towards the centre of the universe, so the probability of success grew ever smaller. It seemed Earth was the only world where life had begun and developed.

Krail had been sent to check whether KZ-917 might be suitable for human habitation. The initial readings on approach had proved positive, so he had begun to go down for a closer orbital check. That was when his ship had suffered a power failure.

Out in the emptiness of space, the repair drones could have rectified the fault—but caught in the grip of the planet's gravity, Krail's exploration ship had begun to fall helplessly towards the atmosphere where it would burn up on entry. He had managed to transmit an emergency signal before taking to the escape capsule.

The capsule had chosen a landing site and set itself safely down on the surface. And now all Krail could do was wait.

And he might have to wait for the rest of his life.

He was a long way from Earth and a long way from any other ship that might be able to rescue him. Finding stranded pilots was not a very high priority, and Krail knew he was expendable. Despite the vast numbers who had emigrated to the new worlds, Earth still had far too many people. No one would miss Krail.

'What do I do now?' said Krail.

He waited for an answer, then realized there would be none. He was on his own. For a moment he'd forgotten that he was in the escape capsule. The computer which had been Krail's only companion had been part of the main ship. The capsule carried only the basic necessities for survival, and that didn't include a computer with a personality of its own.

'What do I do now?' he repeated.

One thing he shouldn't do, he realized, was start talking to himself. That would mean he was going crazy, and the only solution would be to swallow a suicide pill.

Krail wondered if he should do that now. It was almost certain he would die here, alone, No one was going to come looking for him. There was a synthesis machine in the capsule, so all his supplies would be recycled for as long as he lived. He could survive for another sixty Earth years—but by that time he'd really be crazy.

There wasn't enough room to stand up straight in the capsule, so his chances of sane survival would have been better if he could have lived outside. But just a glance at KZ-917 in the light of its two moons was enough to convince Krail that this was impossible. There hardly seemed a level area anywhere. The capsule had found the only piece of flat ground in sight, and there was a deep twisted valley to one side, a towering jagged mountain peak to the other. The area around his ship was filled with weird spiralling shapes, about the size of a man. These could only have been lumps of rock, worn away by the severity of the climate.

Everything was covered in ice. Krail couldn't have lived for long outside without his survival suit. Already the hull of the capsule was glazed with thick white frost, which was beginning to spread over the lens of the periscope, blocking out Krail's view of the sky, the two moons and the stars.

It also masked the inhospitable world where he was stranded, and that was the one thing for which he was grateful.

Krail wondered why all the primary readings he had taken of the planet had proved positive, but he supposed that a small difference in temperature was not very significant. Human beings could live here, just as they lived in Antarctica. Mankind was very adaptable. But as an individual there was no way that he could make even a small part of this world habitable. He simply didn't have the equipment. All he could do was stay inside the escape capsule.

Perhaps in generations to come KZ-197 would be settled, and the capsule would be found below the ice, his body frozen inside, and the new inhabitants would wonder who he was. There seemed very little chance that the planet would be named after him. Krail's World.

He smiled for a moment at the idea, allowing his eyes to close. There was nothing else to do, and he drifted towards sleep. Krail opened his eyes suddenly. Something was different, he sensed, although he had no idea what it was. He turned his head and leaned towards the periscope. Immediately he squeezed his eyes shut and pulled away because of the brilliant light. Turning the dimmer, he looked again.

The ice had gone from the lens, although there were still a few drops of water left. As he watched, even these evaporated in the intense heat. The sun had come up—a huge ball of red fire so bright that Krail couldn't even glance at it when the lens was darkened to its limit.

Instead he spun the periscope, aiming it on the ground around the

ON

ZOOM

MAGNIFICATION

x2   x3   x4

escape capsule. And he could hardly believe what he saw.

Before his eyes, the planet was changing.

The whole world seemed to be dissolving, and for a few seconds Krail couldn't work out what was happening. Then he realized that the ice was melting. The intense heat from the sun was changing the entire landscape. Torrents of water rushed down the mountain and poured into the deep valley below, where a sudden river appeared. The frost that had covered the ground had all gone, and the sterile whiteness had become a patchwork of colourful vegetation—greens and pinks and yellows. The shapes which Krail had supposed to be rocks stood revealed as low trees, and fresh leaves had begun to grow from the stark branches.

It was like watching a speeded-up film, the events of weeks compressed into a few brief seconds.

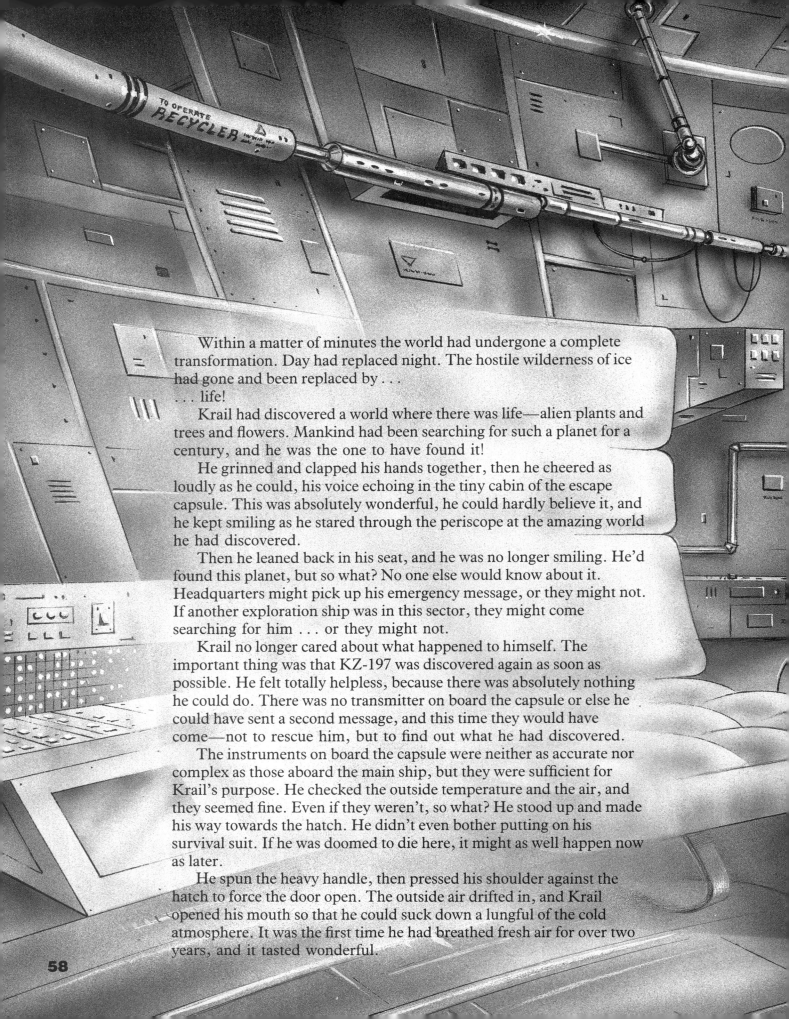

Within a matter of minutes the world had undergone a complete transformation. Day had replaced night. The hostile wilderness of ice had gone and been replaced by . . .

. . . life!

Krail had discovered a world where there was life—alien plants and trees and flowers. Mankind had been searching for such a planet for a century, and he was the one to have found it!

He grinned and clapped his hands together, then he cheered as loudly as he could, his voice echoing in the tiny cabin of the escape capsule. This was absolutely wonderful, he could hardly believe it, and he kept smiling as he stared through the periscope at the amazing world he had discovered.

Then he leaned back in his seat, and he was no longer smiling. He'd found this planet, but so what? No one else would know about it. Headquarters might pick up his emergency message, or they might not. If another exploration ship was in this sector, they might come searching for him . . . or they might not.

Krail no longer cared about what happened to himself. The important thing was that KZ-197 was discovered again as soon as possible. He felt totally helpless, because there was absolutely nothing he could do. There was no transmitter on board the capsule or else he could have sent a second message, and this time they would have come—not to rescue him, but to find out what he had discovered.

The instruments on board the capsule were neither as accurate nor complex as those aboard the main ship, but they were sufficient for Krail's purpose. He checked the outside temperature and the air, and they seemed fine. Even if they weren't, so what? He stood up and made his way towards the hatch. He didn't even bother putting on his survival suit. If he was doomed to die here, it might as well happen now as later.

He spun the heavy handle, then pressed his shoulder against the hatch to force the door open. The outside air drifted in, and Krail opened his mouth so that he could suck down a lungful of the cold atmosphere. It was the first time he had breathed fresh air for over two years, and it tasted wonderful.

Then he jumped down. The surface was soft and damp from the melted ice. Krail stood up straight and stretched out his arms. He hadn't been out of his spaceship or capsule in almost a year, since he had surveyed LC-954, and it was good to have the earth beneath his feet.

No, he corrected himself. Not the earth, but the ground.

The alien sun felt warm on his bare face and hands, even though it was now hidden by thick white clouds that covered the sky. The sun had melted the ice, but the clouds that had appeared protected the vegetation from being dried up.

The escape capsule seemed tiny compared to the sheer walls of mountain and bottomless crevasses which surrounded it. Except for the ledge where the frail craft had set itself down, there was barely a centimetre of level ground in sight. But every slope was now dotted with the bizarre plants. They had thrust themselves from beneath the surface only minutes before, yet looked as though they had always been there. All the ice had gone, sunk into the ground or carried away by the flash floods. Far below, a few pools of water lay trapped among the rocks in the deep ravine to Krail's side, while near the bottom of the steep gorge he could see what appeared to be the entrance to a cave.

He wondered how long a day would last here. There hadn't been time to check earlier, although that would have been part of the computer's final report on the planet. How far could he explore before icy nightfall?

The best thing would be to stay close to the capsule today, then tomorrow he could take a proper look at his surroundings. Tomorrow? Depending how fast KZ-197 spun about its axis, a day could last for months and months. Perhaps he had simply happened to land when it was almost dawn. In his own solar system, a day on Venus was the same as two hundred and forty-three Earth days.

Krail made his way to the nearest tree, a handful of metres away. It was as tall as he, but with two trunks twisting around each other, leaning first one way and then the other, with dozens of spindly branches shooting in every direction, fresh leaves everywhere.

He reached out and touched one of the diamond shaped green leaves. Krail knew little about botany, but the tree didn't look much different from those which could be found on his own world.

The tree was a living thing, and this was the first time a human had ever come across a form of life which had not originated on Earth. Krail knew that the moment ought to feel special, because it was unique in the whole of history.

Today would go down in the record books, or it ought to, but right now that didn't seem important. All that mattered was that it was he who had arrived on KZ-197 first, he who had breathed the air and set foot on the planet before anyone else. His whole life had led to this instant, and the fact that he might be trapped here forever was of no importance.

Krail let his right hand rest on the tree, where the two trunks split and went their separate ways, his fingertips feeling the texture of the alien bark as he gazed off in the distance.

Abruptly he stood up straight, blinking. He'd seen something move across the sky. He stared, but whatever it was had vanished behind one of the distant mountain peaks.

He waited, hardly daring to breathe, watching for the thing to appear again. After a few seconds he thought he must have been mistaken and he started to turn away—then he saw it again. Nearer, coming towards him.

His emergency signal had been picked up, he thought, and another exploration ship was here to rescue him. He couldn't suppress his delight. He jumped up and down, waving his hands above his head.

'Here I am!' he shouted. 'Hey! Over here!' It made no sense waving, he realized, because the ship would be homing in on the escape capsule. But he felt so good that he couldn't contain his elation.

He spun around in a circle and punched his right fist into his left palm as he stared into the sky again—and realized that he was wrong.

It wasn't an exploration ship he had seen, but something else. He didn't know whether he ought to feel disappointed or even more excited, because what he could see flying through the air was a bird.

This was life, true life. Not mere vegetation, but flesh and blood life . . .

Krail watched in awe as the bird drifted through the sky, its wings lazily beating every now and then to keep itself aloft. Although it was difficult to judge how far away it was and its size, the creature seemed quite large, with a wingspan of about two metres.

All the time it was coming closer and flying lower, as though it was heading directly towards Krail. He didn't move, not wanting to scare it away, not even blinking in case it should vanish.

Then it banked to the side and dropped down, landing on a crag of rock about two hundred metres from the man. It was too far away for Krail to see properly, and there was nothing in the capsule he could use to improve his vision. All he could do was try and get nearer.

Although only two hundred metres away, there was no direct route Krail could take because of the deep ravine which separated him from the creature. He would have to cross over to the other side. There was no way of telling how far he'd have to go around before the gorge ended, and the only solution was to climb down and then up the other side.

It was a long way to the bottom as he looked down, although the sides were not as steep as he had first supposed. The rock wall was full of fissures, which offered plenty of footholds. He told himself this was crazy, for by the time he reached the other side the bird would probably have flown away again. But he couldn't miss such an opportunity, and so very cautiously he began scrambling down the rocky slope.

Although he had kept himself fit on board the exploration ship, by the time he was halfway down he was sweating and panting for breath, his uniform had been torn by needles of rock, and his fingers were cut and had begun to bleed.

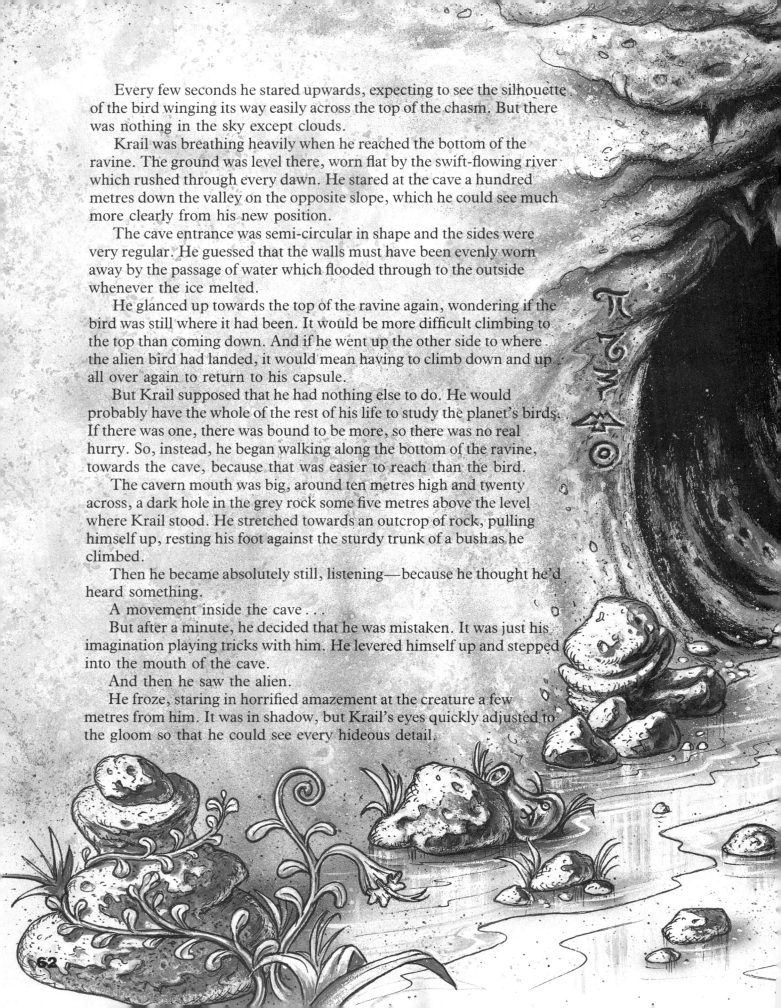

Every few seconds he stared upwards, expecting to see the silhouette of the bird winging its way easily across the top of the chasm. But there was nothing in the sky except clouds.

Krail was breathing heavily when he reached the bottom of the ravine. The ground was level there, worn flat by the swift-flowing river which rushed through every dawn. He stared at the cave a hundred metres down the valley on the opposite slope, which he could see much more clearly from his new position.

The cave entrance was semi-circular in shape and the sides were very regular. He guessed that the walls must have been evenly worn away by the passage of water which flooded through to the outside whenever the ice melted.

He glanced up towards the top of the ravine again, wondering if the bird was still where it had been. It would be more difficult climbing to the top than coming down. And if he went up the other side to where the alien bird had landed, it would mean having to climb down and up all over again to return to his capsule.

But Krail supposed that he had nothing else to do. He would probably have the whole of the rest of his life to study the planet's birds. If there was one, there was bound to be more, so there was no real hurry. So, instead, he began walking along the bottom of the ravine, towards the cave, because that was easier to reach than the bird.

The cavern mouth was big, around ten metres high and twenty across, a dark hole in the grey rock some five metres above the level where Krail stood. He stretched towards an outcrop of rock, pulling himself up, resting his foot against the sturdy trunk of a bush as he climbed.

Then he became absolutely still, listening—because he thought he'd heard something.

A movement inside the cave . . .

But after a minute, he decided that he was mistaken. It was just his imagination playing tricks with him. He levered himself up and stepped into the mouth of the cave.

And then he saw the alien.

He froze, staring in horrified amazement at the creature a few metres from him. It was in shadow, but Krail's eyes quickly adjusted to the gloom so that he could see every hideous detail.

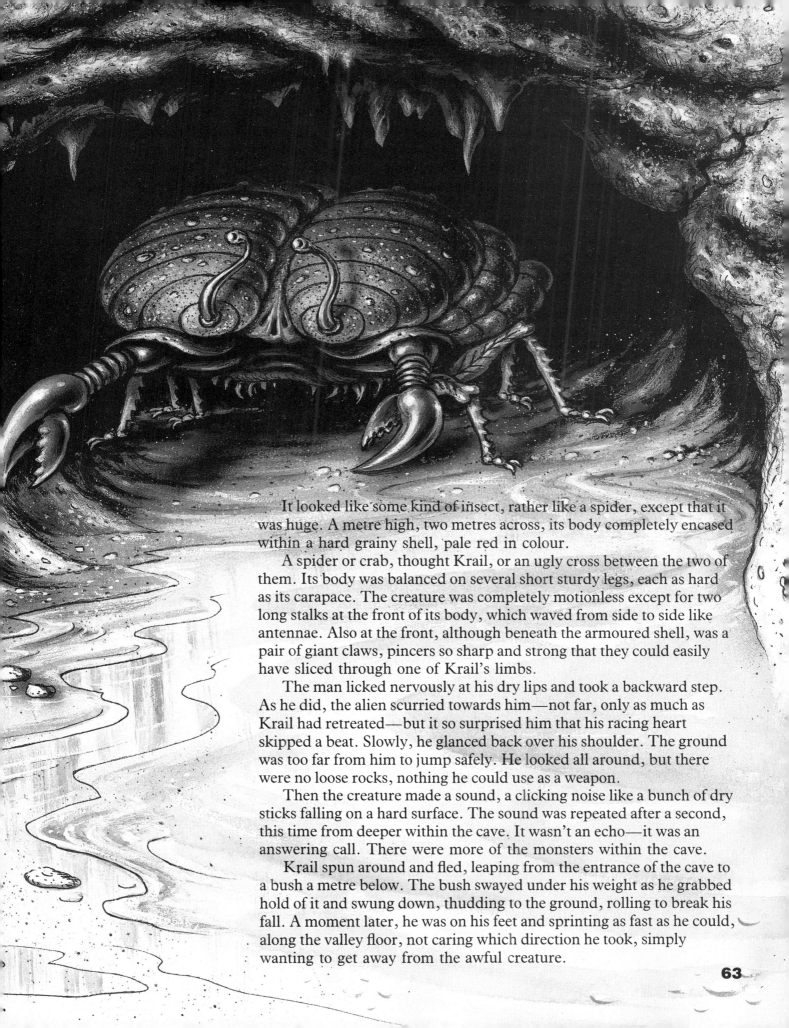

It looked like some kind of insect, rather like a spider, except that it was huge. A metre high, two metres across, its body completely encased within a hard grainy shell, pale red in colour.

A spider or crab, thought Krail, or an ugly cross between the two of them. Its body was balanced on several short sturdy legs, each as hard as its carapace. The creature was completely motionless except for two long stalks at the front of its body, which waved from side to side like antennae. Also at the front, although beneath the armoured shell, was a pair of giant claws, pincers so sharp and strong that they could easily have sliced through one of Krail's limbs.

The man licked nervously at his dry lips and took a backward step. As he did, the alien scurried towards him—not far, only as much as Krail had retreated—but it so surprised him that his racing heart skipped a beat. Slowly, he glanced back over his shoulder. The ground was too far from him to jump safely. He looked all around, but there were no loose rocks, nothing he could use as a weapon.

Then the creature made a sound, a clicking noise like a bunch of dry sticks falling on a hard surface. The sound was repeated after a second, this time from deeper within the cave. It wasn't an echo—it was an answering call. There were more of the monsters within the cave.

Krail spun around and fled, leaping from the entrance of the cave to a bush a metre below. The bush swayed under his weight as he grabbed hold of it and swung down, thudding to the ground, rolling to break his fall. A moment later, he was on his feet and sprinting as fast as he could, along the valley floor, not caring which direction he took, simply wanting to get away from the awful creature.

63

There was no animal like it on Earth, no insect or crustacean of such mammoth dimensions. Krail had discovered life, true alien life, but that seemed of little importance at the moment. All he wanted to do was escape.

His feet pounded against the hard ground and through the puddles of water as he ran, then suddenly he skidded to a halt. There was another one of the things directly ahead of him, blocking his route and coming closer. Turning, Krail saw that the first one was down on the valley floor and in steady pursuit. They couldn't move very fast, but they didn't need to—they had him trapped.

The only way to escape was upwards, and so Krail hurried to the side of the gorge and began frantically to climb, heading back towards his capsule. Once inside, he'd be safe.

His boots scrabbled against the rocks, his fingers clawing for a handhold. He forgot his tiredness and pain. There would be time to worry about those later—if he survived this ordeal.

Slowly, surely, he inched his way up the slope. He didn't want to glance down, but he couldn't help it. The two aliens were directly below him, and they had halted side by side.

Then one of them continued the chase—and it climbed the steep slope as easily as it had scuttled along the level ground. With so many feet it could easily find a grip. This was its world. Millions of years of evolution had adapted the creature to surviving on a planet where so much of the terrain was almost vertical.

Krail didn't have a chance of escape. The being was almost on him, its clicking voice becoming louder and louder, its lethal pincers closer and closer . . .

But a moment before the beast reached Krail, the man missed his footing. He tried to dig his hands into the sheer rock face in an effort to stop himself from slipping, but it was futile.

He shouted out in desperation as he slid down the rocks, then tumbled backwards through the air to the ground.

He lay without moving, all his breath knocked out of him, and he stared up at the sky far above. The shadow of one of the aliens fell across him, and then there was blackness.

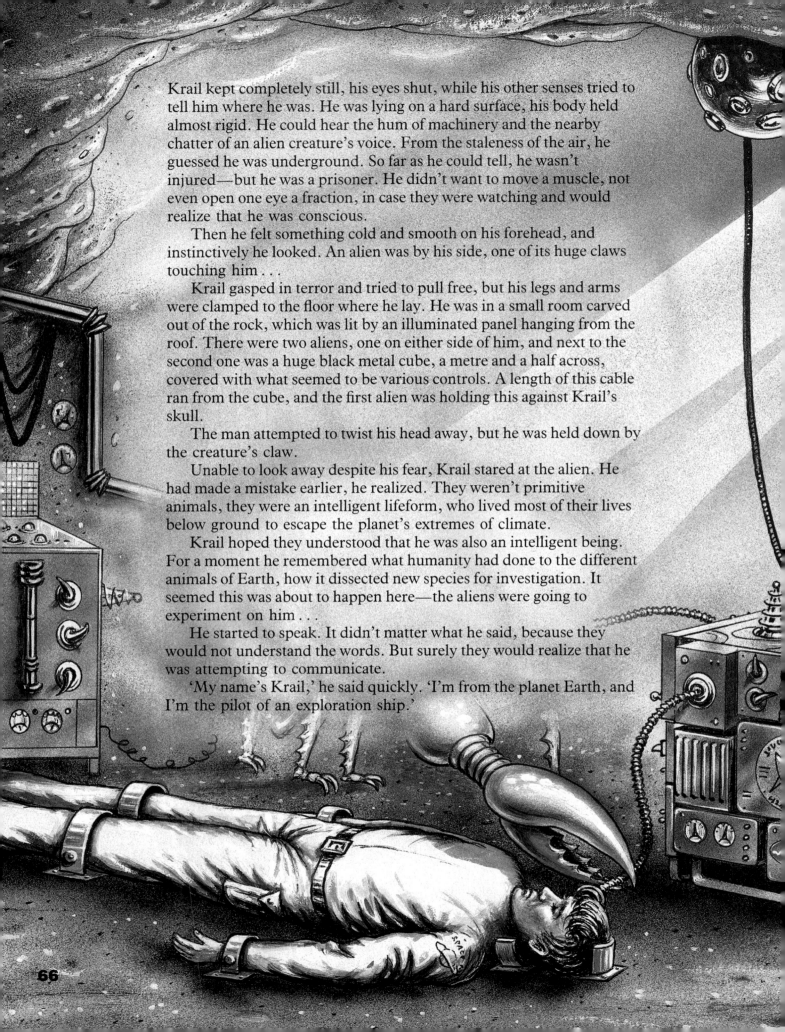

Krail kept completely still, his eyes shut, while his other senses tried to tell him where he was. He was lying on a hard surface, his body held almost rigid. He could hear the hum of machinery and the nearby chatter of an alien creature's voice. From the staleness of the air, he guessed he was underground. So far as he could tell, he wasn't injured—but he was a prisoner. He didn't want to move a muscle, not even open one eye a fraction, in case they were watching and would realize that he was conscious.

Then he felt something cold and smooth on his forehead, and instinctively he looked. An alien was by his side, one of its huge claws touching him . . .

Krail gasped in terror and tried to pull free, but his legs and arms were clamped to the floor where he lay. He was in a small room carved out of the rock, which was lit by an illuminated panel hanging from the roof. There were two aliens, one on either side of him, and next to the second one was a huge black metal cube, a metre and a half across, covered with what seemed to be various controls. A length of this cable ran from the cube, and the first alien was holding this against Krail's skull.

The man attempted to twist his head away, but he was held down by the creature's claw.

Unable to look away despite his fear, Krail stared at the alien. He had made a mistake earlier, he realized. They weren't primitive animals, they were an intelligent lifeform, who lived most of their lives below ground to escape the planet's extremes of climate.

Krail hoped they understood that he was also an intelligent being. For a moment he remembered what humanity had done to the different animals of Earth, how it dissected new species for investigation. It seemed this was about to happen here—the aliens were going to experiment on him . . .

He started to speak. It didn't matter what he said, because they would not understand the words. But surely they would realize that he was attempting to communicate.

'My name's Krail,' he said quickly. 'I'm from the planet Earth, and I'm the pilot of an exploration ship.'

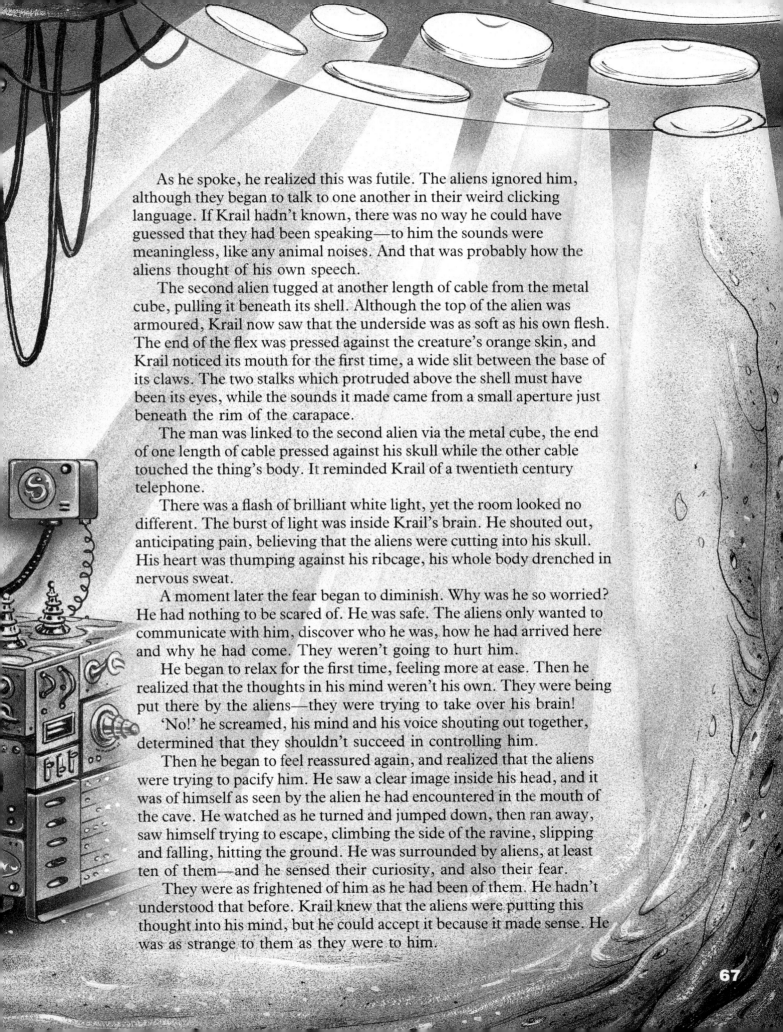

As he spoke, he realized this was futile. The aliens ignored him, although they began to talk to one another in their weird clicking language. If Krail hadn't known, there was no way he could have guessed that they had been speaking—to him the sounds were meaningless, like any animal noises. And that was probably how the aliens thought of his own speech.

The second alien tugged at another length of cable from the metal cube, pulling it beneath its shell. Although the top of the alien was armoured, Krail now saw that the underside was as soft as his own flesh. The end of the flex was pressed against the creature's orange skin, and Krail noticed its mouth for the first time, a wide slit between the base of its claws. The two stalks which protruded above the shell must have been its eyes, while the sounds it made came from a small aperture just beneath the rim of the carapace.

The man was linked to the second alien via the metal cube, the end of one length of cable pressed against his skull while the other cable touched the thing's body. It reminded Krail of a twentieth century telephone.

There was a flash of brilliant white light, yet the room looked no different. The burst of light was inside Krail's brain. He shouted out, anticipating pain, believing that the aliens were cutting into his skull. His heart was thumping against his ribcage, his whole body drenched in nervous sweat.

A moment later the fear began to diminish. Why was he so worried? He had nothing to be scared of. He was safe. The aliens only wanted to communicate with him, discover who he was, how he had arrived here and why he had come. They weren't going to hurt him.

He began to relax for the first time, feeling more at ease. Then he realized that the thoughts in his mind weren't his own. They were being put there by the aliens—they were trying to take over his brain!

'No!' he screamed, his mind and his voice shouting out together, determined that they shouldn't succeed in controlling him.

Then he began to feel reassured again, and realized that the aliens were trying to pacify him. He saw a clear image inside his head, and it was of himself as seen by the alien he had encountered in the mouth of the cave. He watched as he turned and jumped down, then ran away, saw himself trying to escape, climbing the side of the ravine, slipping and falling, hitting the ground. He was surrounded by aliens, at least ten of them—and he sensed their curiosity, and also their fear.

They were as frightened of him as he had been of them. He hadn't understood that before. Krail knew that the aliens were putting this thought into his mind, but he could accept it because it made sense. He was as strange to them as they were to him.

In his mind he could see himself being carefully picked up by two of
the aliens. They carried him back to the entrance of the cave, passing
his unconscious body up to another two who clung to the sides of the
slope, then to another pair at the edge of the cavern. There he was set
down in the back of a strange bulbous multi-wheeled vehicle, which
drove him deeper beneath the surface of the planet.

Then there was a picture of his escape capsule, and the image stayed
before his eyes for a long while. He could sense the curiosity of the alien
who was linked with him, and so Krail concentrated hard, focusing all
his attention on imagining his exploration craft, how he'd been forced to
abandon it and come down to the planet's surface.

And he knew that he was being understood. His original idea about
the metal cube and its lengths of cable, that it resembled a telephone,
had proved correct. It was a communication device which operated by
thought. He was speaking telepathically with one of the aliens . . .

It was hard to concentrate his mind so narrowly, and after a few
seconds he had to stop.

Another image came into his mind, a spaceship. It was like no exploration craft Krail had ever seen, bigger, not so sleek, but he was aware immediately that it served the same purpose.

Just as humans explored the galaxy for other worlds, different life, so did the aliens. And like mankind, they had found none—until now, when Krail had suddenly appeared on their world.

Summoning up all his mental strength, Krail sent out a probe of his own, searching into the alien mind. He found fear and doubt.

The aliens were afraid. Afraid of Krail and of this other spacefaring race which he represented.

He could imagine the panic if the situation were reversed, if, instead, one of them had arrived on Earth. It could easily be viewed as the first step towards an invasion. The alien might be tortured to reveal information—or at the very least killed immediately.

Krail tried to send a message of reassurance, but he didn't know how. It would take time before his mind became adept at using the aliens' communicator, and all he could hope was that they would allow him to live long enough to master it.

It was difficult to measure time underground, and the aliens lived a longer day than Krail was used to. But as near as he could calculate, he had been on the planet some six months by the time the spaceship was ready.

During those six months, as he'd suspected, no other exploration ship had come looking for him—or if one had, the aliens had kept the information from him.

His initial fear that they would kill him had lessened over the months, but every moment he felt as though he had to be on his guard. Human and alien were so totally different that he could never know what they really thought or what their true intentions were.

Krail didn't have a name for the race whose world this was, because their communicator would only carry images or emotions, not words or translations. Neither did he know the names of the handful of creatures with whom he'd shared his mind, although he had given them all nicknames and could easily recognize them.

They were all there when Krail stepped out of the ground car which had brought him to the alien ship in which he would be leaving the planet. But he would not be alone. One of the aliens would be going with him.

They didn't want Krail to leave by himself, and neither could he have flown one of their ships. The idea was that he should return to the nearest human world and that his alien companion would act as an ambassador to establish friendly relations between the two races. No details had been worked out, so Krail and the alien pilot would simply have to take things as they came.

It would be a difficult task to find an inhabited planet, because all Krail's star map co-ordinates had been lost when his exploration ship was destroyed but he knew the best direction to take, and their vessel was well provisioned. Space was big and empty, which was why human and alien exploration ships had never encountered one another.

Today was one of the few occasions when Krail had been above ground, and he saw that the alien craft was balanced on a wide stretch of land which had been carefully levelled. The ship had been brought above the surface soon after dawn. The launch control rooms were deep below ground.

Krail had been on board the ship a few times while it was being prepared, but he had not met the alien who was to be his companion before, and he watched as he arrived in another vehicle. Six months ago the creature would have looked like all the others, but now Krail could tell that he was a male who had reached maturity a long time ago. The man knew that his companion had once been a space pilot, later becoming some kind of politician. Like so many things, Krail hadn't been able to work out how the alien world was run or operated, despite all the images of assemblies and debates which had passed through his mind. It all seemed as dull as government back on Earth.

The alien took no notice of Krail as he climbed out of his ground car and walked towards the gantry which supported the ship and began to climb towards the hatch. Krail glanced around at the beings near him, shrugged, then also made his way to the ship.

At the top of the gantry, he turned and looked at the strange planet again—the soaring mountains and the plunging valleys, the clouds which obscured the sun for most of every day. Then he waved to those below, although he knew they wouldn't respond, and he ducked his head to enter the low hatch. He secured the door behind him.

There were two couches side by side in the nose of the ship, one shaped for a human, one for an alien. Between them was a communication box. The pilot was already seated, waiting for take-off, and Krail hauled himself to the top of the ship and took his place. The alien's eyestalks turned to look at the man, then one of his claws reached for the communicator cable.

Krail took hold of the other cable, pressing the end against his forehead, slowly opening up his mind to his companion, trying to pick up the creature's thoughts.

And the initial image was of repulsion, the image of a soft and vulnerable animal. This was how the alien thought of him, as ugly and frightening.

For a moment Krail was angry, then he remembered his own first reaction on encountering the aliens—that they were hideous and vile. It was still something he couldn't shake out of his head, no matter how illogical.

He shook his head and smiled, and he laughed briefly because it was so funny.

Then he heard a strange noise coming from the alien, a light chattering sound which he had never heard before.

His mind was still linked with the pilot, and so he knew immediately what the noise was—alien laughter. His companion had picked up Krail's thought about how ugly the aliens looked to the human.

Side by side, as they waited for the countdown, Krail and the alien both laughed and laughed.

And at last Krail had no doubts. He knew he and pilot were going to get on together—as was mankind and the alien race.

The universe was a big place. But human and alien would be friends as well as neighbours.

Aliens and Planets

a game by Douglas Hill

The aliens of planet KZ–917, in David Garnett's story, are perfectly adapted to the harsh terrain of their world, yet have also managed to develop an advanced civilization. On this page are pictures of six more equally harsh and dangerous planets, where other kinds of intelligent alien beings can be found. Some of these beings are quite civilized, while others are more or less primitive—on pages 95/96 we have shown each alien on its own, without any possessions or other objects that might be a giveaway. Can you fit each alien to the world that it comes from? Mark your choice in the A & P box on page 95 then check the answers on the same page.

The planet **Freinyn**: a scorched and waterless world, because part of its orbit takes it too close to its huge, stormy sun. Its alien inhabitants are primitive nomads who are perfectly capable of surviving the blazing heat of their cruel desert land.

The planet **Chrhrhr**: a world of dense and riotous forest, or jungle, particularly dangerous because of the long snaky vines, with their vicious thorns, that grow everywhere. The vines can move, wrapping themselves around other creatures, stabbing with the thorns and feeding on their victims' blood. But the aliens who live here, intelligent and fairly civilized, have a special way of protecting themselves.

72

The planet **Icta 5**: a world of terrifying cold, where mountains and valleys, plains and oceans, are all covered with gleaming ice many kilometres thick. Yet intelligent beings developed even here—aliens that are unaffected by cold, equipped to live comfortably on and beneath the endless ice.

The planet **Vlmis Ato**: an ugly, stinking world of swampy mud and foul water, with hardly a square metre of solid ground. Yet many forms of life exist here, including quite civilized alien beings entirely at home amid the muck and slime.

The planet **Poenintce**: a jewelled world, where the land and all its living creatures are formed of colourful, glittering crystals. And so are the highly intelligent and highly civilized aliens who dominate the planet.

The planet **Harenmn o Hae**: a world that never evolved past its violent volcanic stage, where life clings on grimly despite the non-stop eruptions of molten lava, ash and flame, steaming water and more. Here too intelligent but fairly primitive alien beings can be found—if you look in the right place.

73

4 Alien Attack

Another of the faint, high, musical sounds, and then another, jolted Russell out of that frozen moment of panic. Scooping up Mizzo's limp body, he dived beneath the heavy table. He knew that even its solid wood would be no protection against the filaments. But at least the table was still intact, so he could be sure that the filaments were not sweeping through that part of the room—yet.

Peering out for an instant from under the table, he glanced up at the ceiling. There were the telltale spots, a scattering of small, dark-metal blobs from which the filaments were bursting out, stretching downwards to the floor. His heart sank as he saw how many blobs there were, and how several of them were directly above the table.

A flare of anger swept through him—

aimed mostly at himself, for having left Mizzo exposed to the enemy. It would have taken Ekridolak only seconds to enter the house, put Mizzo out of action, and fling the dark blobs at the ceiling. They would now be solidly fixed—so that Russell could not pull them off, even if he survived long enough to climb on to the table and try.

Across the room, a sturdy wooden chair collapsed suddenly, sliced neatly into two halves by the unseen, swinging deadliness of a filament. Before Russell's eyes, a deep gouge appeared in the carpet, as the tip of another filament slashed through its fibres.

Desperately, knowing he might have only seconds left, Russell struggled against panic, trying to make himself calm enough to think. He reached into his memory for anything that he knew about the planet Krasti, where the filaments had been developed.

A hot, dry planet, he recalled, desolate and waterless. Yet highly civilized, with strange stony cities rising from the desert, and even stranger alien beings living in them. They had impossibly thin, dry, many-armed bodies, rather like large and distorted stick insects. But they were the most skilled micro-engineers in the galaxy, and the filaments were only one of their startling inventions.

A small, half-formed thought tried to make itself noticed in Russell's mind. But two or three more of the faint musical notes had sounded, meaning that more filaments had been released. And a new wave of fear blocked his thoughts for a moment, when a corner of the heavy tabletop above him was suddenly lopped off, as if by a silent and invisible axe.

Russell dragged his gaze away from the damaged table, in time to see another long slash appear in the carpet, only half a metre away from him. It extended across the room, almost reaching the bucket of water that he had carelessly forgotten to empty . . .

The half-formed thought burst fully into life within his mind.

It was a chance, he thought feverishly. He might be killed trying it—but he would soon be chopped to pieces anyway, where he was.

Without a second's hesitation, he plunged out from under the table. His body was braced against the slashing impact of a filament, and he imagined that he could feel them, sweeping through the air around him. But he remained unharmed in the two seconds that it took him to leap across the room.

the water struck, the dark blobs
d into hissing clouds of steam. Within
am Russell could see the blobs
g, dissolving, dripping like thin silty

Then his weary thoughts were disturbed, by a weak but sharp voice from under the table. 'A messy way you have chosen, to clean the house.'

Russell crouched joyfully, and saw Mizzo trying to drag himself to his feet. 'You're alive!'

'How observant you are,' Mizzo said sourly. 'But I do not feel lively. I feel ill, and my head aches, and I wish I had never left home.'

'What happened?' Russell asked.

Mizzo hissed angrily. 'Ekridolak happened. He burst in with a vapour-gun, and gassed me before I could move. From then I remember nothing. What happened to you?'

Russell quickly told him about the filaments, and how he had managed to put an end to them. 'Lucky for you,' he said at last, 'that you're not as warm-blooded as Earth

And in his mind's eye was the image of the baking, desolate, *waterless* deserts of Krasti—as he snatched up the bucket, and with desperate strength flung its contents at the ceiling.

It drizzled most of the time during the next day, Monday, and the clouds were still heavy and grey by evening. And the weather exactly suited Lindy's mood, as she wandered slowly along the pavement, dragging her feet, trying not to look across the street at the curtained windows of Russell's house.

Ever since they had left that house, Lindy and Jeff had been trying not to look at it or think about it. But it was an impossible task. They had not been able to turn their minds to anything else, throughout Sunday, and neither of them had slept very well that night, their minds full of nightmares about black, hairy monsters from space.

In the morning, when they met outside their homes to go to school together, they had been listless and tense at the same time. They were unable to attend to their schoolwork, which irritated their teacher. And, after school, they had still been unable to settle to anything, which exasperated their parents. Lindy had picked at her food, had found her mind wandering too much to be able to read or watch TV, and so had finally slipped out to go over to Jeff's, where at least they could be miserable together.

It was just too much to bear, she thought to herself. Here we've made the most amazing and wonderful friends we'll ever make—and at the same time, those friends are in deadly danger. For all she knew, Russell and Mizzo might be lying dead or injured, right at that moment, inside that silent house. But all she and Jeff could do was

hedge by a neighbour's gate. But then the blur could be seen more clearly. It was the shaggy, dark-haired, floppy shape of Mutt, Jeff's dog. And Mutt came towards her, tongue lolling and tail wagging as usual.

Lindy stopped and waved her hands [in] shooing motion. 'Go away, Mutt,' she sa[id] crossly. 'Go on—clear off!'

As usual, the tail-wagging stopped. [But] also as he usually did, the dog kept com[ing,] brown eyes gazing up at her, head stretc[hed] forward to sniff at her.

Lindy went very still, as if she had t[urned]

She took a shuddering breath, and forced herself to turn her head. The dog was ambling slowly along the pavement across the street, in a perfectly ordinary way. As Lindy watched, it turned the corner, and was hidden from her sight by the thick hedge that grew there. The hedge that grew along the side of Russell Carron's house, and his back garden.

The dog's disappearance seemed to release Lindy from her frozen stance. She sprang forward into a frantic sprint towards Jeff's house. And less than two minutes later, both children erupted out of the house, hardly hearing the voice of Jeff's mother telling him to be home before dark. Jeff's face was just as pale with shock as Lindy's— because Mutt, his dog, was flopped in a shaggy black heap in his basket indoors, and had been there all evening.

But despite their fear, the faces of both children also looked fiercely determined.

'We can't just go in,' Jeff muttered, as they came to a halt by the hedge at the side of Russell's house. 'We could get in their way, and make things worse.'

'I know,' Lindy said. 'But we have to do *something*! We have to!'

Jeff gulped, and summoned his courage. 'Let's go into the garden,' he said, 'and have a look. Maybe that alien won't try anything if it knows we're around.'

Neither of them mentioned the strong chance that the shape-shifting alien might deal with them as murderously as it intended to deal with Russell and Mizzo. Slowly, tremblingly, they pushed their way through a small gap in the hedge, and stared around.

Russell's small back garden was empty, looking as ordinary and innocent as ever. But the hearts of both children seemed to stop beating when they saw that the back door of the house was standing slightly open.

'That thing . . . it's gone *in*!' Lindy whispered.

'Maybe we should call our dads, or something,' Jeff said nervously. 'Or the cops.'

'We promised to keep Russ's secret!' Lindy protested. 'No matter what!'

Again Jeff swallowed, and nodded, and the two children looked at each other. They were both sweaty and shaky, more frightened than they had ever been in their lives. But they knew, without having to say it, that they could not simply turn and run.

'Let's look inside,' Jeff said. 'See if anything's happening.'

As quietly as they could, they moved towards the door that stood slightly ajar. From within the house they heard a faint sound—like a voice, saying words they could not understand, in a soft, menacing growl. The sound turned both children icy cold, and lifted the hairs on the backs of their necks. Yet, even so, they found the courage to pull the door farther open, and to creep silently into the empty kitchen of the house.

Their shoes noiseless on the smooth floor, they tiptoed across the kitchen, to the doorway that led into the main living room. The low growls from that room had stopped, and the house seemed filled with a tense and threatening silence. Carefully, fearfully, Lindy and Jeff peered round the edge of the doorway, into the living room.

And there they froze, held rigid in the grip of a terror so overpowering that they could not even find the breath to scream.

FIND OUT WHAT IS HAPPENING IN THAT OTHER ROOM BY TURNING TO PAGE 84.

Can *you* SURViVe on an aLieN PlaneT?

Answer Box

Mark your
choice of action here

△ 9	⑩ 10	☐ 11

The NIGHT .....

9

NIGHT HAS FALLEN BY THE TIME
YOU LEAVE THE ALIEN FOREST.
YOU FIND YOURSELF ON A
SLOPE LOOKING UP AT A STRANGE
OBELISK AT THE TOP OF THE HILL

WILL YOU STEP FORWARDS UP
THE SLOPE TOWARDS YOUR GOAL? (A)

WILL YOU WAIT AWHILE TO GAZE AT
THE BRILLIANT STARLIT SKY? (B)

IF YOU ARE CARRYING THE **NIGHT GLASSES** YOU
MAY USE THEM TO SPY OUT THE SKY (SEE PAGE *15*)

10

YOU HEAR A RUSTLING NOISE
SOMEWHERE JUST AHEAD.
YOU HESITATE AND PEER AHEAD
IN THE GLOOM.

WILL YOU MOVE TO THE LEFT? (A)

WILL YOU MOVE STRAIGHT AHEAD? (B)

WILL YOU MOVE TO THE RIGHT? (C)

IF YOU ARE CARRYING A **TORCH**
YOU MAY USE IT (TURN TO PAGE *15*).

11

YOU WILL NOT BE ABLE TO
SIGNAL FOR HELP UNTIL DAWN
AND WILL HAVE TO CAMP IN THE
OPEN ON THIS ALIEN HILLSIDE.
BUT WHERE WILL YOU BE SAFE?
THE NIGHT CREATURES OF
ABETHAZE WILL BE HUNTING
FOR YOU.

WILL YOU CAMP NEAR THE OBELISK? (A)
WILL YOU CAMP NEAR THE GIANTGRAZER? (B)
WILL YOU CAMP NEAR THE DARK CLUMP OF VEGETATION? (C)
WILL YOU CAMP UNDER THE ALIEN TREE? (D)

IF YOU ARE CARRYING THE **NIGHT GLASSES** YOU MAY
USE THEM TO SPY OUT THE LAND AHEAD. (SEE PAGE *15*.)

9A

AN EARWING HEARS YOU MOVE AND SWOOPS OUT OF THE DARKNESS TO ATTACK YOU. IT GASHES YOUR SHOULDER DEEPLY IN ITS FIRST FEROCIOUS PLUNGE. YOU MANAGE TO TAKE COVER BEFORE IT CAN DIVE AGAIN BUT *LOSE 13 SURVIVAL POINTS*.

9B

YOU WATCH THE SKIES AND SEE THE DARK SHADOW OF AN EARWING HUNTING. THEY USE THEIR HUGE EARS TO FIND THEIR PREY AND SO THEY HUNT IN THE SAME WAY NIGHT OR DAY. YOU WAIT UNTIL THE VICIOUS CREATURE HAS FLOWN AWAY BEFORE MOVING ON.

10A

YOU HAVE STEPPED IN A MOUTHPLANT. YOUR LEG IS TRAPPED AND THE MOUTHPLANT WILL NOT LET GO. IF YOU HAVE A **KNIFE** OR A **LASER**, YOU CAN CUT YOURSELF FREE BUT *LOSE 19 SURVIVAL POINTS*. IF YOU HAVE AN UNUSED **MEDIKIT** THEN ONLY *LOSE 9 SURVIVAL POINTS*. IF YOU HAVE NO **KNIFE** OR **LASER** THEN YOU ARE TRAPPED FOREVER AND WILL EVENTUALLY BLEED TO DEATH ON THIS ALIEN HILLSIDE.

10B

YOUR FOOT COMES DOWN ON TOP OF A SHELL-CREEP. THE FRIGHTENED CREATURE GRASPS YOUR ANKLE. IF YOU ARE WEARING THE **EVA BOOTS** YOU SUFFER NO HARM AS THE CREATURE'S TENTACLES CANNOT GRIP. IF NOT *LOSE 8 SURVIVAL POINTS*.

10C

IF YOU DON'T HAVE A **TORCH** YOU STEP GINGERLY TO THE RIGHT AND STUMBLE OVER A SMALL BUSH AND FALL FLAT ON YOUR FACE! BUT NO DAMAGE DONE. THE BUSH IS QUITE HARMLESS. YOU GET TO YOUR FEET FEELING A BIT OF A FOOL, BUT ALIVE AND WELL.

IF YOU HAVE A **TORCH** YOU STEP OVER A HARMLESS BUSH AND CONTINUE ON YOUR WAY UP THE HILL.

The NIGHT ....

11A

YOU MAKE CAMP AT THE SUMMIT NEXT TO THE OBELISK. THIS IS FAIRLY SAFE BUT VERY UNCOMFORTABLE. FLOCKS OF POISONBILLS FROM THEIR NEARBY ROOST CONSTANTLY OVERFLY THE OBELISK DRAWN BY THE LIGHT OF ITS GHOSTLY GLOW. THE OBELISK PREVENTS THE POISON BILLS FROM LANDING BUT YOU LIE AWAKE ALL NIGHT IN AGONY AS ACID DROPPING FROM THEIR BILLS BURNS YOUR CLOTHES AND SKIN. *LOSE 4 SURVIVAL POINTS* OR NO POINTS IF YOU STILL HAVE A MEDIKIT.

IF YOU ARE STILL ALIVE GO TO THE OBELISK (SEE PAGE 93).

11B

YOU DECIDE TO CAMP NEAR THE GIANTGRAZER HAVING REALIZED THAT THIS TERRIFYING LOOKING CREATURE EATS ONLY VEGETABLE MATTER. UNFORTUNATELY FOR YOU THE GIANTGRAZER USES ITS LIGHTS TO ATTRACT THE SHRIEK-HOUNDS WHICH HELP IT BREED. AS YOU APPROACH, THE HOUNDS TURN ON YOU. THEY DON'T LIKE THE ALIEN TASTE OF YOU MUCH. BUT THEY CHEW YOU ENOUGH TO CAUSE CONSIDERABLE DAMAGE. *LOSE 27 SURVIVAL POINTS*. FOR EACH MEDIKIT YOU HAVE LEFT, *LOSE 9 POINTS LESS*. IF YOU ARE STILL ALIVE GO TO THE OBELISK (SEE PAGE 93).

11C

YOU SEE THAT THE ONLY DANGER IN THE CENTRE OF THE SLOPE IS FROM A NEST OF FLOWERTEETH. THESE CARNIVOROUS PLANTS NEST TOGETHER AND CANNOT MOVE DURING THE NIGHT. IT WILL BE QUITE SAFE TO CAMP HERE UNTIL DAWN. BUT YOU MUST BE UP AND AWAY BEFORE FIRST LIGHT AS THE FLOWERTEETH WILL START TO MOVE AS SOON AS THE SUN IS IN THE SKY. IF YOUR SURVIVAL POINTS TOTAL IS BELOW 20 THEN YOU ARE SO WEAK AND TIRED THAT YOU FAIL TO WAKE IN TIME. YOU BECOME AN EARLY BREAKFAST FOR THE FLOWERTEETH AND YOUR ADVENTURE ENDS HERE. IF YOU GOT UP IN TIME THEN GO TO THE OBELISK (SEE PAGE 93).

11D

YOU HAVE BEEN FOOLISH ENOUGH TO CAMP UNDER A POISON-BILL ROOST. AS SOON AS YOU FALL ASLEEP HUNDREDS OF THE BIRD-CREATURES LAND ON YOU AND ATTACK YOU WITH THEIR ACID SPITTLE. THERE ARE TOO MANY OF THEM AND YOU NEVER WAKE UP AGAIN. SOON THE VICIOUS BIRD-CREATURES HAVE PICKED YOU CLEAN, NOTHING REMAINS BUT YOUR BONES.

5 Sentinel on EARTH — The Shape-shifter

The interior of that room confronted the horrified children with a scene from nightmare.

The alien killer, Ekridolak, stood in the centre of the room, in his true form—a squat, shapeless mass of tangled black hair. But his yellow eyes glowed cruelly from within the matted hair over his face. And a short, powerful arm extended from the shaggy mass, its clawed hand gripping a strange, small object of silvery metal.

The monster did not see the two children, standing silent and frozen in their terror. Nor had Russell or Mizzo noticed them. Mizzo was slumped on the floor, and Russell was half-lying in a chair across the room, both unable to move.

They were held in the grip of something that looked like netting, or over-sized cobweb. It seemed sticky and damp, and was a sickly white colour—and it clung tightly around its two victims, pinning their limbs. A small drop of the same sticky white substance clung to the tip of the object in Ekridolak's hand, showing that the object had somehow *fired* the ghastly web at the two captives.

As both Russell and Mizzo struggled hopelessly against the clinging strands, the killer's other hand emerged from the tangle of hair. It held a long, slim, glittering blade—but it was no ordinary knife. The blade seemed to be a blur, as it vibrated at an unbelievable rate. And it hummed faintly, sounding like it was charged with strange electrical forces.

Ekridolak raised the blade, so that it could be clearly seen by his victims. And Russell, held fast by the web, gazed at it with eyes that seemed entirely calm and unafraid.

'*Sentinels*!' The word burst from Ekridolak like a vicious spit of contempt, in that same growling voice that the children had heard before. 'How can you guard a planet of primitives when you cannot protect yourselves? I knew you would be too cowardly to fight me. But I did not think even you would be so foolish as to *remain* here, after your fortunate escape from the filaments.'

The words were spoken in an alien language, meaningless to the children. But Russell understood—and his eyes narrowed slightly as the alien killer took a menacing step forward, and spoke again.

'You will die now,' Ekridolak growled, 'and your bodies will vanish. Later the fools of the Inner Accord may send as many Sentinels as they wish, for I will have taken what plunder I desire from this backward world.'

He took another step forward, the knife sweeping forward in a glittering arc. The children could hardly breathe, as if their very bodies were being squeezed in that grip of terror. They could see nothing but the evil glinting blur of that vibrating blade.

They had not noticed that the room had been rearranged slightly, nor that for some reason the large refrigerator had been brought in from the kitchen. They had not noticed that Russell also held a strange object in his right hand—an object no larger than a doorknob, covered with strange raised markings.

Nor did they notice when, even within the grip of the clinging web, Russell's long fingers moved slightly, sliding over the object that they held. But the children certainly did notice, with astonishment, when two totally unexpected things happened.

The refrigerator door slammed open, and from it came a one-second burst of icy air, as bitingly frigid as an Arctic gale. At the same instant, from the other side of the room, the stereo system erupted with an equally short blare of ear-jangling sound, a discordant crash that shook the walls and made the children stagger as if they had been struck.

Under the impact of that blast of icy air, the clinging web that gripped Russell and Mizzo turned black, and shrivelled, and broke away, like the tendrils of a vine turned brittle in a sudden frost.

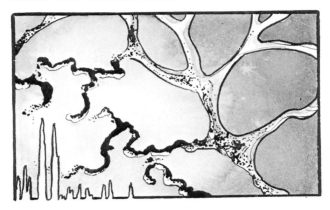

And under the impact of that deafening crash of sound, the quivering knife-blade exploded into dust, as one set of vibrations met another, destructively.

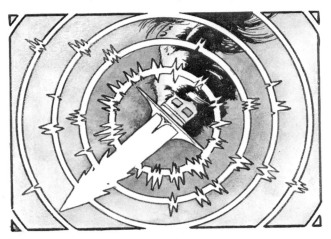

In the instant of their sudden freedom, Mizzo spat a searing jet of flame just past Ekridolak's other hand, which still held the object that had fired the web. The killer jerked his hand back, and the object spun out of his grip, clattering to the floor. And Russell was lunging up from the chair, diving to retrieve the fallen weapon.

But he was not quick enough. Ekridolak's other hand moved almost too fast for the eye to follow, plucking another weapon from somewhere within the mass of tangled hair. From that weapon—small, metallic, bulbous—flared a wide and spreading beam, of lurid blue. The beam caught and held both Russell and Mizzo.

And both of them stiffened, as rigid as statues in the positions that they had held when the beam struck.

'You are cleverer than I expected,' Ekridolak growled. His voice now held a note of cruel gloating, as he held the ugly weapon steady, still bathing his victims in that baleful ray. 'Clever to guess what weapons I would bring against you, and to adapt these primitive machines to protect you. But you cannot save yourselves from a paralyser.' His laughter was a savage snarl. 'I need only increase the power of the paralyser—and your hearts will stop beating, your lungs will no longer take in air.'

Slowly, as if enjoying the cruel suspense of the moment, he brought his other hand around, to alter the controls on the bulbous weapon that was the paralyser.

The two watching children in the doorway had not understood the alien words. But they recognized the evil laughter, and from the sudden flare of distress in Russell's eyes, they guessed what was happening. And in that monstrous, desperate moment, they found that their own silent paralysis—of terror—was no longer strong enough to grip them, in the face of their more overpowering fear for their friends.

'No! *Don't!*' they shrieked, as one.

Ekridolak was skilled enough to keep his hand steady, holding the paralyser beam on his victims. But his head jerked around, the yellow eyes ablaze with shock at the unexpected interruption, and the sight of the two children.

And their terror grew almost unbearable—as they watched the killer's shaggy body quiver, and blur, as it changed its shape.

But as Russell had told them, the shape-shifting ability among Ekridolak's people was a protection, a defence. So it operated on the level of instinct, as an automatic *reflex*, as when a human jerks his hand away from a fire.

Ekridolak had turned to find two Earthlings confronting him, cutting off his escape through the door. Before his mind could tell him that they were only children—and before his brain could use the paralyser or another weapon on them—his shape-shifting *reflex* had been triggered.

And because one of them was Lindy, whom he had passed some moments ago, on the street, Ekridolak automatically shifted into the same shape that he had taken before.

Where there had been a menacing alien holding a strange and lethal weapon, the children suddenly found themselves looking at the familiar hairy form of Mutt, Jeff's dog.

And dogs . . . have no hands.
The paralyser clattered to the floor, its beam switching off.

And this time Russell was quick enough. Before Ekridolak could change again, back to his own shape or to some other, Russell completed the dive that had been halted by the paralyser beam. He snatched up the first weapon that the killer had used, and fired.

Ekridolak, still in his dog form, was lunging with bared fangs at the children. But he was halted—by a spreading mass of sticky white web, wrapping itself around him in an unbreakable grip.

The two children huddled in the doorway, trembling, trying hard to keep from crying with relief and the effects of shock and terror. And Russell stood looking down at them, with a strange mixture of feelings in his expression.

'I thought I asked you two to stay away from this house,' he said quietly.

'It is lucky for us they did not,' Mizzo said. He had picked up the paralyser, and was holding it idly, watching Ekridolak with unblinking violet eyes. The killer—in his own shape again—lay glaring and snarling, firmly held in the clinging bonds of the web.

'You could have got yourselves killed,' Russell went on, to the children.

'Could have,' Mizzo said sharply. 'But killed we *would* have been, Rasl, if they had not distracted Ekridolak. It is thanks we owe them, not a scolding.'

'I'm not scolding,' Russell said mildly. He reached out to let his hands rest on the children's shoulders—then stooped quickly and put his arms around them, hugging them tight. 'We do owe you thanks. A great deal. You were very foolish, and very brave.'

In a moment or two the children stepped back, sniffing loudly and blinking moist eyes. 'What will you do with him?' Jeff asked, glancing at the bound killer.

'We'll wait for dark, and for my ship to be in the right place,' Russell said lightly. 'Then we'll take him for a walk in the garden.'

He explained to the children about his orbiting spaceship, and the Transplacer beam. The force field created by the beam would take Ekridolak—still bound by the web—up to the ship. But the field would remain switched on, within the ship, an unbreakable cage that would keep Ekridolak prisoner.

'My ship is already programmed,' Russell said. 'It'll set off for one of the planets where our friend is wanted, for all his crimes. And the peace force of that planet will be alerted by the Sentinels, to pick him up.'

Lindy looked worried as a thought struck her. 'Couldn't he change shape and get out somehow?'

'He cannot,' Mizzo explained. 'He changes shape as a reaction to danger. But now the danger has already *happened*, and he is captive. Too late now for the reaction to be set off.'

'Wish we could stay and watch the force field take him,' Jeff said. 'But we have to be home before dark.'

'Very wise,' Mizzo said with a hiss of laughter. 'Bad things might happen to you, crossing the street after darkness.'

The children giggled weakly at the absurd thought that their peaceful street could offer any danger, compared to what they had seen in that room.

'Russ, do you think,' Lindy asked hopefully, 'you might take *us* up to your spaceship sometime?'

'Why not?' Russell said. 'As long as we can find a way to do it secretly.'

The eyes of both children shone with excitement. 'When?' Jeff asked eagerly.

Russell shrugged. 'Sometime soon. Of course, the ship will be away from Earth for several days, delivering Ekridolak to that other planet.'

'And in that time,' Mizzo put in acidly, 'the ship will not be monitoring space around the Earth. So we must hope that other alien intruders do not come too soon, prowling and threatening.'

The children looked anxious at that, but Russell grinned. 'We don't need to worry too much,' he said. 'If other aliens come, we'll be all right till the ship returns.' He ruffled the hair of his two young friends, who smiled up at him. 'I think that the *four* of us can handle just about anything that comes along.'

Sentinel of EARTH — THE END.

Did you survive on an alien planet?!   Rescue?

You wake to the silence of a magnificent dawn on Abethaze.

You have with skill survived for a day and a night on the most dangerous planet in the galaxy. But you realize you mustn't push your luck too far – somehow you have got to get help before even worse Abethazian lifeforms attack you.

You examine the strange obelisk that you have been making for. It is clearly the work of an intelligent civilization but it is lifeless and opaque.

Do you have the **Subspace Distress Beacon** with you? If not you are doomed to end your days here on Abethaze. Sooner or later one of the deadly lifeforms will get you – it may be matter of days, hours, minutes . . . or even seconds.

If you do have the Distress Beacon then you press the orange button. To your astonishment the obelisk next to you turns transparent in response to a red beam and exerts a high-pitched sound. It is in fact a Rescue Crystal programmed to respond to radio signals. It has been placed here by the Abethazians in case they are ever stranded in the wild parts of their planet. It will deter any lifeforms from coming close and will call for help. You can wait safely for your rescue. Check your Survival Points and see how you compare with the Space Academy survival standards.

Aliens and Planets

Match these six aliens to their correct home planets on page 72,
then check your choices on the opposite page